JENNY PENDLETON

There was no question of her being about the prettiest girl he had ever laid eyes on. He had been struck by this the minute he saw her standing out in that backyard with the lantern light on her face. And then, after they got home, he had caught himself staring at her in the kitchen. And when she looked back at him he felt a crazy kind of embarrassment he had never experienced before.

Later, he slowly wrote her name on a blank pad, **Jenny**. It was an important day in his life. He finally returned the pad to the desk drawer, climbed into bed and switched off the lamp. He listened but could hear no sounds from the girls' room. He smiled, picturing Jenny's hair spread across the pillow as she slept. He hoped she liked it here . . .

BANTAM PATHFINDER EDITIONS

A comprehensive and fully integrated series
designed to meet the expanding needs of the
young adult reading audience and the
growing demand among readers of all ages for
paperback books of high quality.

Bantam Pathfinder Editions provide the best in
fiction and nonfiction in a wide variety of
subject areas. They include novels by classic
and contemporary writers; vivid, accurate
histories and biographies; authoritative works
in the sciences; collections of short
stories, plays and poetry.

Bantam Pathfinder Editions are carefully
selected and approved. They are presented in a
new and handsome format, durably bound and
printed on specially selected high-quality paper.

THE WALTONS

ROBERT WEVERKA

Based on the television series
created by Earl Hamner, Jr.

BANTAM PATHFINDER EDITIONS
TORONTO / NEW YORK / LONDON

RLI: $\dfrac{\text{VLM 6 (VLR 6–8)}}{\text{IL 5–adult}}$

THE WALTONS
A Bantam Book / published December 1974

Published simultaneously in the United States and Canada

Bantam Books are published by Bantam Books, Inc. Its trade-
mark, consisting of the words "Bantam Books" and the por-
trayal of a bantam, is registered in the United States Patent
Office and in other countries. Marca Registrada. Bantam
Books, Inc., 666 Fifth Avenue, New York, New York 10019.

PRINTED IN THE UNITED STATES OF AMERICA

I

It had been an unusually cold winter. From Christmas through the middle of March the ground was frozen and the barren trees stood like charred skeletons in the biting frost. It was a difficult time for Olivia Walton. Washing had to be strung across the kitchen and back porch to dry, and the weather forced the children inside and underfoot most of the time.

The demand for firewood was brisk, and John Walton kept busy. But hauling logs down from the mountain was a cold and finger-numbing task, as was delivering it after it was cut. John-Boy helped, and Grandpa Walton bundled himself up and pitched in as much as he could. The days were short, but seemed long, and in those bitter mornings John Walton no longer bothered looking at the thermometer.

Still, the evenings were pleasant and cozy. With the smells of damp wool and Grandma Walton's pastries in the oven, the children did their homework by the fire while Olivia sewed and Grandpa chuckled quietly or

1

carried on one-sided conversations with the voices on the radio.

The first signs of spring came in early April. Crocuses seemed to magically appear in full blossom; the first buds of green became visible on the alder and mulberry trees, and farmers could be seen plowing their fields under bright sunshine. John-Boy Walton watched, and marveled at the incredible power of nature in the changing season. How many millions of seeds were responding to this first warmth of spring? And how many billions of leaves would be coaxed and drawn from their frozen hibernation into the lush green landscapes of summer? And like the trees and the flowers, the people of Walton's Mountain shed their protective mittens and heavy coats and once more seemed alive.

Spring vacation came in the second week of April. On the last Friday of school Miss Hunter was lenient with those who had not fully prepared their lessons. She overlooked the daydreaming and giggles and restless talking, and when the hour for dismissal came she wished them all a happy Easter and stood carefully away from the door to avoid the squealing, clattering rush into the sunshine.

John-Boy Walton had no special plans for the week. The last thing he expected to do was fall in love, or get mixed up with the law and a wholesale bootlegging operation. As far as John-Boy knew there would only be the usual chores, and he would help his mother start a vegetable garden. And he would do some writing. Springtime seemed particularly suited for poetic thoughts. And he would read—Mike Timberlake had agreed to trade his copy of *The Good Earth* for John-Boy's *The Deerslayer*.

"Beats me why you wanta read a book about China," Grandpa observed when John-Boy set out for Mike Timberlake's house, " 'pears to me all them Chinamen ever do is grow rice and have more babies."

"The book won the Pulitzer Prize, Grandpa."

"Won the Pullet Surprise, did it? Well, can't be much of a book if the best it can do is win a chicken."

It was one of Grandpa's favorite jokes and he was always delighted with an opportunity to use it.

It was growing dark when John-Boy started home from the Timberlake house. The nights were still chilly, and with the book clamped under his arm and the collar of his jacket turned up he hurried past the church and up the road toward the old Pendleton house.

John-Boy had only a dim recollection of the Pendleton family. Eight or nine years ago when he was about Jim-Bob's age, everyone always moved very quietly past the Pendleton house, and spoke only in whispers. Mrs. Pendleton was sick and permanently confined to her bed, which made her existence seem frighteningly mysterious to their immature minds. And the Pendleton girl was extremely shy and never spoke of her mother, which heightened the mystery. It also stimulated fertile imaginations: Mrs. Pendleton had two heads, each with a single eyeball in the middle of the forehead. Others claimed to have peered through the window and seen a raving beauty with long blond tresses—her arms and legs securely chained to the bedposts.

The fact was, John-Boy learned years later from his father, Mrs. Pendleton was a very nice woman who suffered from a lung disease, and her husband had finally moved her to the warmer climate of Florida. But with the house vacant all these years, and with the weeds growing thicker and the paint now totally gone, the place still served as a perfect setting for tales of witches and ghosts and goblins. John-Boy smiled at those recollections as he hunched his shoulders against the cold and glanced up at the shuttered windows of the old house. It was easy to imagine creaking doors and rattling chains and wisps of vaporized spirits floating up the dusty stairways. After all these years there could be thousands of ghosts inside, crowded into dark closets, bumping into each other, laughing and planning—all anxiously waiting for Halloween to go out and terrorize the children of Walton's Mountain.

John-Boy's upward glance was brief. It swept vaguely across the upper windows and then back to the

dark road in front of him. Then his heart leaped into
his throat and he stopped breathing for a moment.

Had he seen something in the window? John-Boy
stopped and looked again.

On the far left, one of the shutters had been partly
torn loose and now dangled crookedly from an upper
hinge. It was there, in that narrow triangle of exposed
glass, that he'd seen the flicker of light.

Or had he? Of course he hadn't—it was impossible.

He stood perfectly still for a minute, staring, his eyes
focused narrowly on the dark window. It was ridiculous to think anyone was in that old house. Still he
didn't move. He watched the window, his senses alert,
listening. But there was nothing.

In the bushes at the side of the house a cricket
chirped furiously and then stopped as abruptly as it
started. But the house stood dark and lonely and silent,
displaying no evidence of light or movement inside.

Could it have been a reflection? John-Boy glanced
down the road and at the fields behind him. There were
no house lights that might have flickered off the win-
dowpane. Nor were there any flashing headlights from
automobiles.

John-Boy stared at the house for another minute and
then laughed to himself as he turned and headed for
home again. The light he had seen in the window was
clearly a product of his own imagination. Thinking
about creaking doors and rattling chains and vaporized
ghosts, it was not surprising that he should imagine the
spirit of Mrs. Pendleton floating through bedrooms
with a candle in her hand. Ten years ago he had half
believed all of those wild stories. And now that he was
old enough to know better, those childhood fears were
coming back to play tricks on him. John-Boy gave the
house one more backward glance and then smiled as he
continued along the road.

While John-Boy was hurrying home that night, the
topic of heated discussion at the Walton supper table
was tadpoles. It was not a theoretical discussion, for
standing squarely in the middle of the supper table was
an old gallon-sized pickle jar containing a countless

mass of the squirming creatures. With Olivia's kitchen strainer Mary Ellen had scooped them all out of the nearby pond and into the confinement of the jar, and they had been placed on the table for the purpose of observation and safekeeping.

Reactions to their presence were sharply divided. Thirteen-year-old Erin, who always arrived at the table with immaculate hands and fastidious manners, protested the most vehemently.

"I don't see how anyone can be expected to have an appetite with those slimy things staring at him all the time. Yuccch!"

"They're not slimy things, and you don't have to look at them."

"How can anybody avoid lookin' at them when you put them right in front of our faces?"

"I think they're fun," Jim-Bob countered. Along with Ben and Elizabeth he had helped Mary Ellen at the pond, and was unable to keep his eyes off the slithering mass. Seated next to him, Grandma had the opposite problem. After one shuddering glance she avoided looking at them at all costs. "I don't see why we have to have the nasty things at the table."

"They're not nasty, Grandma."

"Huh! If those things aren't nasty, I don't know what is."

"If you like them so much, why don't you just put them on your plate with your supper," Erin said with disgust.

After ten minutes of such debate Olivia decided it was time for compromise. "Mary Ellen, I really don't think it's necessary to have them on the table. Couldn't you put them out of sight until we're through?"

"Aw, gee, Mama—" but she quickly gave up the protest in the face of Olivia's firm smile. She placed the jar at her feet and contented herself with surreptitious downward peeks, along with some sharply disapproving glances at Erin.

Grandpa had finished his meatloaf and pulled back his cuffs for the ritual of cutting his corn from the cob. "What're you goen to do with all them polliwogs anyway, Mary Ellen?"

"Start a bullfrog farm."

"I never heard of such a thing. You gonna plant 'em?"

"Of course not, Grandpa. We're gonna let 'em grow into frogs and get rich. Just like Elwood P. Fairweather."

"Never heard of a rich frog," Grandpa smiled. "You say his name is Elwood P. Fairweather?"

"Oh, Grandpa!" Mary Ellen said over the laughter.

John Walton had smiled with amusement through the initial controversy. Now he looked curiously at Mary Ellen. "Who in the world is Elwood P. Fairweather?"

"Elwood P. Fairweather just happens to be one of the richest men in the world. And he made about six hundred million dollars sellen bullfrogs' legs to restaurants. I read about him in *Liberty* magazine."

"I don't believe it," Erin said haughtily.

"You'll believe it when all the people with restaurants in Charlottesville and Richmond come beggen us to sell 'em frogs' legs."

"We're gonna make a million dollars," seven-year-old Elizabeth said gravely.

Ben nodded. "We've already caught almost a hundred of 'em."

"And we're goen to get another hundred tomorrow," Mary Ellen added.

"If you think you're goen to keep a hundred bullfrogs in our room," Erin said, "I'm moven out."

"I'm just gonna keep the tadpoles there till they turn into bullfrogs."

"Yes, and they'll probably be hoppen all over the room. Suppose I have to get up in the middle of the night. You want me to step on one?"

"I just told you, I'm only—"

"All right," Olivia said gently, "I think it's time we called a truce. And I think it would be a good idea if you kept the pollywogs outside somewhere, Mary Ellen."

Any protest was cut short by Reckless's sudden barking outside the back door. It was not the sound of alarm, but his half-moaning, half-squealing bark of happy welcome. A moment later the screen door slammed and John-Boy came in.

Olivia rose to get the warming meatloaf from the oven. "I don't appreciate your bein' late for supper, young man. Get yourself washed up."

"I'm sorry, Mama."

"Where you been, son?" John asked.

"I was over at Mike Timberlake's getten a book. I guess I didn't see how late it was."

"Get that chicken winner, did ya?" Grandpa asked.

"Yes, I did, Grandpa." John-Boy washed quickly, then spotted the tadpole jar as he sat down. "What're those for?"

"That's dessert," Grandpa laughed. "For the last person to finish supper."

"We don't need no more talk like that, old man," Grandma said and rose to help clear the table.

"Daddy?" John-Boy asked, filling his plate. "Do the Pendletons still own that old house down the road?"

"Far as I know Dave Pendleton still owns it. His wife died a few years ago. Why?"

"I just wondered." Now that he was home John-Boy was more certain than ever that his eyes had been playing tricks on him. "Seems crazy to leave that house empty and let it just fall apart like that."

"Well, I guess Dave figured to come back sometime. I been keepen an eye on it for him all these years."

"The place is haunted, you know," Grandpa said.

John grinned. "That's what they say. Guess that's as good a way as any to keep people away from it."

"I shouldn't wonder," Grandma sighed, "considerin' all the tragedy that house has seen. That poor Laura Pendleton all consumptive an' everythen. It was a mercy she died."

John-Boy ate in silence while the others finished clearing the table.

"You could bring in some wood for the stove after supper, John-Boy," John said. "And I expect you and me could be getten another half cord cut up before bedtime, Grandpa."

Grandpa nodded, but neither of the men made a move to rise. They had worked hard all day, and nobody questioned a man's right to relax a few minutes after supper before he returned to work.

Much of the wood they cut now would be stacked and allowed to dry out for next winter, while the better logs would be fine-cut for building purposes. Not that there was much building going on in Walton's Mountain, or even over in Charlottesville. The way things were, a man was lucky he wasn't being foreclosed and evicted, much less planning on building something new. But barns and fences and roofs had to be repaired, and John Walton liked to have lumber stock on hand if the opportunity arose to sell it.

Grandpa stretched, sat back, and gazed thoughtfully over at Olivia, who had returned to scrubbing clothes. "John," he said. "When you goen to buy Livvy one o' them new washin' machines?"

The question was asked casually, as if Grandpa didn't really expect a serious answer. But John-Boy saw the quick shadow pass across his father's eyes. Considering that an accumulation of four or five dollars cash at any time was a rarity, a new washing machine was out of the question. John glanced at Olivia and smiled grimly.

"Grandpa, it's about all I can do right now to put food on this table."

Olivia laughed and picked up another dirty shirt. "I wouldn't know how to work one of those things anyway, Grandpa."

"You could learn, couldn't you, Mama?" Jason asked from the sink.

"Oh, I reckon I could, Jason. But what's the use wishen for things you can't have?"

John-Boy suddenly felt a pang of sympathy for his father. Grandpa had meant nothing by the question—he was only making conversation. But John-Boy could feel his father's embarrassment and the frustration at not being able to buy his family all the things he might have wished.

When the new Sears & Roebuck catalog came just before Christmas, the whole family had gone through it page by page marveling at the clothes and appliances and toys and machinery. But none of them—except maybe Elizabeth—seriously expected to get any of those things. The brand name of the washing machines was Water Witch, and they had all looked admiringly at the gleaming white pictures of the Good, Better, and Best models until his mother insisted they move on. Olivia Walton, more than any of them, knew the foolishness of hopeless dreams.

"Well," Grandpa said, "as long as we're wishen, I think I'll take one o' them new Packard motorcars. With yellow paint. How 'bout you, John?"

John Walton was thoughtful for a minute, then he pushed his chair back. "I think I'll take Livvy, Grandpa." He grinned and crossed the room. "Why, scrubbin' clothes ain't so bad. How do you think this pretty little girl keeps so skinny? Look at her! After given us seven thoroughbred children, why she's still got a figure like an eighteen-year-old!"

"Oh, John, don't be silly! John, you're gonna get yourself all wet!"

He lifted her hands from the tub of soapy water and hoisted her from the floor, swinging her by the waist.

"That's right, Livvy, girl. And now I'm gonna kiss the prettiest thing that ever came down the turnpike!"

"John!" She held him off with one hand, but couldn't stop herself from giggling as he finally planted a big kiss on her mouth and swung her around again.

The dishwashing had stopped and they were all watching as Grandpa slapped the table with a grin.

"Lord a'mighty," Grandma said, "the goens-on in this house!"

"Now I got the strength to go back to work," John announced, "Grandpa, give Grandma a kiss so's you can be some good out there in the mill."

Grandma gasped and headed for the living room. But whether it was deliberate or not, she didn't move fast enough. Grandpa caught her arm and pulled her down.

"Disgraceful," she said when she broke away.

"Old lady," Grandpa called after her, "if the good Lord hadn't wanted us to be kissin' all the time he'd have fixed it so we couldn't pucker! Ain't that right, John-Boy?"

John-Boy smiled sheepishly and carried his dirty plate to the sink. "Well, I guess I'd better be getten that stovewood in."

"Good night, John-Boy."
"Good night, Mary Ellen."
"Good night, Elizabeth."

The good-nights echoed through the house, each of the eleven family members saying "Good night" to ten others until John Walton's long, sleepy yawn signaled an end to the day. Then he kissed Olivia tenderly.

"I really don't want one of those washen machines," Olivia told him. She too had seen the look on John's face when Grandpa mentioned the subject.

"Well, some day you're goen to have one whether you like it or not, Livvy. Things are gonna get better."

She smiled and moved closer to him, feeling a desire for nothing more than the husband and family that she already had. But she knew the washer was very important to John.

In Jason, Ben, and Jim-Bob's room, Jason smiled with sleepy amusement as Ben explained to Jim-Bob in hushed whispers how they would put advertisements in all the newspapers and people from all over the world, even Texas, would send money to buy their frogs' legs.

In the girls' room, Erin listened closely for telltale sounds indicating the presence of hidden polliwogs while Mary Ellen and Elizabeth fell asleep with dreams of multiplying frogs' legs.

John-Boy lay with his hands behind his head and listened to the sounds of the night. Somewhere a bedspring creaked and then was silent. From the girls' bedroom he could hear hushed whispering that finally tailed off, and then he quietly switched on his light and looked at his writing pad.

His notes from last night were about Grandma and Grandpa. He had seen them sitting on the porch yesterday afternoon and had written:

*Grandpa is half dozing and Grandma is quietly knitting
socks, and Grandpa has reached over and touched her
hand for a couple seconds. Neither of them has spoken
or looked at the other, but somehow the gesture seems
very profound. It says more than any poem or song
could ever say, and in spite of Grandpa's bad jokes and
Grandma's pretenses of irritation they share a great
deal of life and love.*

John-Boy reread the notes, then put the pad away
and switched off the light without writing more. But he
thought about his mother and father for some time before going to sleep. As long as he could remember his
father had worked twelve hours a day, and still they
had very little in the way of comforts to show for it.
They were poor, just as everyone else in Walton's
Mountain seemed to be poor. The Depression—some
mysterious activities of bankers and politicians in
Washington and New York and Richmond—seemed to
deprive the Waltons and everybody else of anything
more than just enough to eat. And for many, his father
had told him, they even had to go begging to get that.

John-Boy knew it was the shadow of this despair he
had seen in his father's eyes at the supper table. And
for an instant John-Boy had felt the frustration as
deeply as his father had. And yet, if they ever got some
money, if some miraculous windfall presented them
with a hundred or even a thousand dollars, the last
thing his mother would permit them to use it for would
be a washing machine.

John-Boy wondered. Maybe it was possible to get
her a washing machine without a miracle. If it could be
done, he guessed it would be about the biggest, most
overwhelming surprise in her life.

II

Ike Godsey's General Merchandise Store smelled of leather and pickles and oil and sawdust and ground coffee, and it was far more than a general merchandise store. Ike Godsey could step behind a caged window and become an authorized agent of the United States Post Office, or if someone was going off to Richmond or Charlottesville on important business, he could dust off his old barber chair and make them look as slick and smell as good as any city dude. And for passing time, there was an open cracker barrel, a potbellied stove, a nickel slot machine, and in the back, a genuine pool table. For the children, a glass-enclosed display offered a breathtaking variety of penny candy.

Forty-eight-year-old Ike Godsey oversaw his domain with a smiling good humor that effectively disguised his sharp trading abilities. Like everyone else in Walton's Mountain, Ike had no money to speak of, but he survived, which was an accomplishment in itself, and he could pride himself on never having once cheated a soul in his business dealings.

This morning his smile was particularly broad, and he followed his two customers around the store with solicitous attention. The customers were the Baldwin sisters: two old maids who had the good fortune of being almost totally unaware that the country was in the midst of a depression. The Baldwin sisters seldom came into Ike's store in person, and their presence foretold purchases of significant quantity.

"Isn't that lovely, sister!" Miss Mamie said, admiring a bolt of floral-patterned material. "Do you think it would be too gay for an evening frock?"

"I just got that in yesterday," Ike encouraged, "all the way from Raleigh. Fine material, Miss Mamie."

"Oh, yes, do buy it, sister," Miss Emily enthused. "And wouldn't it make lovely curtains!"

Of the two sisters, Miss Emily was the more daring and often wore feathers or satin-bodiced gowns that would have scandalized her sister if she were to appear so attired in public. Miss Emily's enthusiasm for the floral print now quickly decided the question in favor of something more conservative.

"I think I'll take four yards of this gray material, Mr. Godsey. It's very dignified, don't you think?"

"Very dignified. Very elegant, Miss Mamie. And particularly suited to a charmin' and beautiful lady like yourself."

It was a plain old silly piece of bald flattery, but still lovely to hear. Mr. Godsey certainly knew how to be a gentleman. Miss Mamie moved to the display of J. & P. Coats thread.

"And how many mason jars will you need today, ladies?" Ike asked.

Mason jars were a staple commodity in Ike Godsey's store. All the ladies of Walton's Mountain did canning, and during the summer and fall heavy supplies of preserves were laid in for the winter months. But the Baldwin sisters' purchases of mason jars were a steady all-year business for Ike. At least once each week, usually on Saturday, they fired up the still in their specially built Recipe room and brewed a supply of the fine old whiskey originally formulated by the late, honorable Judge Morley Baldwin.

There was no commercial taint to the Baldwin sisters' activities. Indeed, it was purely tradition; a desire on the part of the sisters to carry on the courtly and mannered graciousness so perfectly exemplified by the life of their distinguished father. No matter what the time of night or day, not to offer any caller or wayward traveler a sip of his famous Recipe, to Judge Baldwin would have bespoken gross ill-breeding. And for the Baldwin sisters not to have carried on this tradition would not only have shamed the memory of their revered father, but Southern Hospitality itself.

"A dozen jars will be fine, Mr. Godsey," Miss Mamie responded.

"Don't forget about Cousin Homer Lee, sister."

"Oh, dear, I forgot about him," Miss Mamie exclaimed. "Yes, you'd better make it two dozen jars, Mr. Godsey. And we'll be needen more grain and malt. And sugar, of course."

Ike made a check of his storeroom. "You got visitors at your place, ladies?" he called out.

"Yes. Fourth cousin Homer Lee Baldwin is visiten from Buckin'ham County. And he *does* love Papa's Recipe."

"Don't think I ever met him. He the one who ran off with that circus sideshow lady?"

"Oh dear, no! That was cousin Clyde. Cousin Homer Lee's a businessman."

Ike came out of the storeroom burdened with cartons. "That so? What business he in?"

"Oh, all sorts of grand business enterprises, Mr. Godsey. I declare, Cousin Homer's been just about ever'where an' done just all sorts of interesten things."

"You must come callen," Miss Mamie added, "I'm just sure you an' Cousin Homer would just have so much to talk about, you bein' in business and all."

"I'd enjoy that, Miss Mamie. Afraid I only got a dozen and a half mason jars right now. But a new delivery ought to be here in a day or two."

"That'll do just fine, Mr. Godsey."

They all looked to the front door as the bell tinkled and John-Boy came in.

"Why, John-Boy Walton, how nice to see you!"

"Mornen, Miss Mamie, Miss Emily."

"Now just look at you," Miss Emily said. "Why, you're getten just as handsome as you can be, John-Boy. And how's your daddy and Mr. Walton? It's just been ages since they've come a-callen."

"They're fine, ma'am."

"You be sure an' tell 'em now that we'd just admire ever so much seein' 'em any time they're out our way."

"Sure will, ma'am."

"And your mama too. It'd be such a pleasure to have her come a-callen some time."

"Yes'm." John-Boy smiled politely, but he had no intention of passing along the invitation. In spite of Judge Morley Baldwin's reputedly superior bloodlines, in the eyes of John-Boy's mother the Baldwin sisters were far from the most upstanding citizens of Walton's Mountain. She would tolerate them, just as she might tolerate a town loafer or a woman who dyed her hair. But she would do so with her back stiff and her lips tight. The gracious traditions of Southern Hospitality were not nearly so important to her as regular attendance at the Baptist Church and strict avoidance of alcohol in all its forms.

The two ladies returned to examining merchandise, and John-Boy moved to the counter where Ike was totaling up figures. He had hoped there would be no other customers in the store so he could talk some business and maybe do some haggling with Ike. But it looked like the Baldwin sisters would be there for some time. And Ike was working hard on the numbers.

"What can I do for you, John-Boy?"

"Oh, nothen much," John-Boy shrugged. He glanced around the store and peered sharply into the back. "Say, Ike . . . a while back didn't you used to have an old secondhand washen machine for sale around here?"

"Still got it, and it ain't so old. It's back there in the corner."

Ike was still working on the figures and John-Boy moved casually to the rear of the store. In doing busi-

ness with Ike Godsey, the worst thing a person could
do was appear eager to make a purchase. John-Boy
found the washing machine under a pile of new coveralls, and knelt beside it. How an electric washing
machine operated was a mystery to him. But the motor
and all the gears and shafts seemed to be in good
shape. The machine was gray, and altogether it didn't
look as sleek as the Water Witches in the Sears & Roebuck catalog. But there were no big dents or scratches.
John-Boy lifted the coveralls enough to peer into the
tub, and then strolled casually back to the counter.

"How much you asken for the old thing, Ike?"

"You getten married an' settlen down, John-Boy?"

"No. I was kinda thinken about it for my mama."

Ike gave him a sly glance and went back to his
figures. "How's thirty-five dollars sound to you?"

"Sounds right steep for a secondhand machine."

"Machine's hardly used at all. Claytons only had it a
couple months before they moved on to Kentucky."

"They got new ones in the Sears & Roebuck catalog
for only fifty dollars."

"Well, John-Boy, I'm in no real rush to sell it, I
reckon."

John-Boy shrugged. "Well, I reckon I'm in no real
rush to buy it either. Not at that price." John-Boy
moved over to a display of hunting knives and studied
them with interest.

" 'Course," said Ike, "seein' as how it's for your
mama, now I might think about letten you have it for
thirty dollars. As is."

John-Boy considered the offer. "I might pay twenty.
But I don't even know if the thing works."

"Oh, it works fine. Slick as a whistle." Ike smiled.
"Twenty-five dollars, John-Boy. That's rock bottom."

"Twenty."

Miss Emily was smiling from one to the other, fas-
cinated by the dickering process. Ike scratched his
head, glanced at Miss Emily, then went back to his
figures. "You're a hard bargainer, John-Boy. Okay, it's
yours. Twenty dollars."

Miss Emily beamed happily, as if she had struck
the bargain herself. "Oh, your mama is just goen to

love that machine, John-Boy. Imagine, a brand-new washer!"

"Yes'm," John-Boy smiled, and turned back to the counter. "There's just one more thing, Ike. I don't have the money right now, and I was kinda hopen I might be able to work it out some way. I could come down here every day after school and make deliveries and do odd jobs for you. And I could be here all day this week, durin' vacation."

Ike stared as if John-Boy had suddenly gone mad. "You want me to give you a job, so's you can get the washer for nothen!"

"I'll work hard, Ike. It's not like you weren't getten somethin' in return."

"I'm sorry, John-Boy. I'd like to accommodate you, but money's short with me, same as ever'body else. An' I'm given you that washen machine for practically nothen as it is."

"You could work for us, John-Boy!"

It took John-Boy a minute to realize what had been said and who said it. Miss Emily had stepped forward and was smiling brightly at him. "We'd be just ever so delighted to have you," she bubbled, "and we've got just all kinds of things you can do! Oh, I just think this is the most wonderful idea! Now, John-Boy, you just wait here a minute while I discuss it with my sister!"

"But, Miss Emily—"

John-Boy gaped with alarm as she hurried off to talk to Miss Mamie. Working for the Baldwin sisters was completely out of the question. Considering his mother's attitude, he might just as well hire himself out to the devil.

Ike was watching the whole thing with a broad grin. "Looks like you got yourself a job, John-Boy."

"But I can't! Mama would skin me alive if she found out I was worken at the Baldwin place."

"Oh, I don't reckon they're gonna have you maken whiskey for 'em, John-Boy. Likely they got somethin' else in mind for you."

"Yes, but—"

It was the last chance John-Boy had to protest. The two sisters were suddenly hurrying over, bursting with enthusiasm. "Why, this is just the most wonderful news, John-Boy! Emily tells me you're goen to help us out, and you're goen to buy your mama a washen machine with all your earnin's!"

"Help from heaven!" Miss Emily chimed in. "An' just when we needed it most! Didn't this just work out perfectly, sister?"

"We have a guest, you see, John-Boy, and—"

"Fourth Cousin Homer Lee Baldwin from Buckin'ham County!"

"He's such a hearty eater."

"We just hadn't heard from him in years, John-Boy. We thought he'd gone into politics. The Baldwins have always excelled at politics, don't you know. But lo and behold, Thursday mornen I opened the door and there he was! Cousin Homer!"

"You sure you really need me, Miss Emily?" John-Boy asked. "I mean, maybe your cousin could help out."

He didn't intend the statement to be humorous, but they both giggled. "Did you hear that, Mamie?"

Miss Mamie shook her head. "Cousin Homer Lee and physical labor just never made each other's acquaintance, I'm afraid, John-Boy."

"Perfectly charmin' gentleman, don't you see," Miss Emily added. "But delicate."

"Got it from his mama, poor boy."

"She wasn't a Baldwin, of course. What could one expect?"

"When will you report for work, John-Boy?"

"Well, I—" John-Boy glanced at Ike and scratched his head. It was hopeless to protest any more. As far as the Baldwin sisters were concerned the matter had been long settled. "Well," he shrugged, "I guess whenever you say, Miss Emily."

"Splendid! And I expect there's no time like the present, is there."

"This will be so nice," Miss Mamie said. "And won't Cousin Homer Lee be delighted. All of those things on the counter there are ours, John-Boy."

The ladies headed for the door and John-Boy gathered the boxes and bags. "Ike, you'll hold that washen machine for me, won't you?"

"Sure will, John-Boy. Unless in the meantime somebody comes in here with cash on the barrelhead."

"But ... suppose I get enough for a down payment?"

"Well, now I reckon that depends on the size of the down payment."

"Yoooo-hooooo!" Miss Emily called from the door.

As quickly as John-Boy got into the car he knew he had made a mistake; that he should have protested more strongly. Still, he didn't know how he could have done it without hurting their feelings. On the other hand, he had no idea how he was going to explain the whole thing to his mother.

The Baldwin sisters' car was a 1921 Franklin that looked as clean and shiny as the first day Judge Baldwin drove it up from Richmond fourteen years earlier. John-Boy squeezed into the back with all the purchases while the ladies arranged their skirts, and Miss Mamie, seated behind the wheel, finally decided they were ready to go.

Once they had made a broad turn, which carried them through a weed patch and back onto the road, Miss Mamie operated the vehicle as if she believed her only obligation was to keep her hat in place and keep a tight grip on the wheel to avoid falling out. Left to its own devices, the car angled to one side until its wheels caromed into a ditch or a plowed field. At that point Miss Mamie, smiling benignly, made a sharp correction and they angled slowly across the road toward the opposite shoulder.

"You're just goen to love Cousin Homer Lee, John-Boy," Miss Emily said. "It's so rare to encounter a true gentleman these days. And my, how he enjoys Papa's Recipe! I do so enjoy seein' a man eat and drink with such vigor, don't you, Mamie?"

Miss Mamie struggled with the wheel, straightened her hat, and sent them back on a leftward course. "It truly is a pleasure, sister. I just can't hardly remember the last time we had a man around the house."

John-Boy held his breath each time they approached the edge of the road. But what concerned him even more was the possibility that he might be seen with the Baldwin sisters, and he kept a sharp lookout for anyone in the fields or walking along the road.

He had no idea what kind of work they had in mind for him, or if it was just for the day or would require him to return several times. If whatever it was could be completed in one afternoon, he could very likely tell his mother about it without her getting too upset. The job would be done and she would see that he had not been corrupted or enticed into evil ways by their famous Recipe.

"Isn't the springtime lovely," Miss Emily was saying. "I just love to see all the little flowers a-blossomen and the birds singen. It's a joy to drive through the countryside again. Don't you think so, John-Boy?"

"Yes, ma'am," John-Boy said. Then for the tenth time he caught his breath as Miss Mamie fought the wheel and set them back on a starboard course.

The original Baldwin mansion had been destroyed in the Civil War. All that remained of the four Grecian columns and gracious verandas were a few stumps protruding from the weed-covered foundations. In a shady grove a few hundred yards beyond the original site Judge Baldwin had constructed a miniature replica of the mansion, and Miss Mamie carefully aimed the car at an open garage attached to the side. She stiffened, her foot against the brake pedal, and the car groaned, shuddered, and bucked, then choked into silence as they came to a perfectly positioned stop inside.

"Well!" Miss Mamie sighed, "wasn't that a delightful drive?"

"I declare, sister, you're getten better every time we go out. Don't you think so, John-Boy?"

"Yes'm."

From the garage, a door opened into a comfortable room, half of which was filled with coils of copper tubing, caldrons, a wood-burning stove, and cupboards. The other half was furnished with leather chairs and low tables, giving it the appearance of a gentleman's study.

"This is our Recipe room, John-Boy." Miss Mamie

smiled. "Did you know we still make Papa's Recipe? It's such a comfort to us, and people come from all over Walton's Mountain just to taste it."

"Yes, ma'am."

"You can bring the supplies in here, and then just come on in and meet Cousin Homer Lee."

The ladies went through a second door, removing their hats, and John-Boy brought the supplies in from the car. He had heard so many stories about the Baldwin sisters' Recipe room he was pleasantly surprised by its homey appearance. He had expected something more like a medieval dungeon with mossy walls and torture racks.

When he finished unloading the car, John-Boy went through the kitchen and followed the sound of voices into the living room, where he had his first view of Cousin Homer Lee.

He was an impressively handsome man, standing casually by the fireplace. His silvery hair reached almost to his collar, and his goatee and string tie reminded John-Boy of pictures he had seen of famous southern senators. He was holding a silver goblet in his hand, chuckling softly as the two ladies giggled.

"Oh, Cousin Homer Lee, you say the nicest things. I declare, I just can't for the life of me understand why you all haven't married in all these years. Can you, Mamie?"

"Ah, the joys of wedded bliss I fear have escaped me," Cousin Homer crooned. "Had I met a young lady with half the charm and beauty of either of my two favorite cousins, no doubt I would today be engulfed in a sea of happy grandchildren."

"Oh, no, I think you're just teasen, Cousin Homer." Miss Mamie blushed. "But I declare those are just the sweetest words to hear."

" 'Scuse me, Miss Mamie," John-Boy said. "I got all the supplies put away. Is there anythen else you'll be wanten me to do?"

"There certainly is, John-Boy. You can just come right in here this minute an' meet Cousin Homer Lee Baldwin from Buckin'ham County! Cousin Homer Lee, this is John-Boy Walton. He's goen to be a writer!"

"Indeed!" Cousin Homer Lee said. He quickly crossed the room and shook John-Boy's hand. "An honor, sir, an honor. I have always held the profession of journalism in the highest regard."

John-Boy nodded, but Cousin Homer continued to pump his hand. "And what line of work are you in, sir?"

"My line of work? Of late, sir, I have been a traveler. A sojourner pursuing commercial activities of varied and diverse natures."

"I didn't know that, Homer Lee!" Miss Mamie exclaimed.

Miss Emily was equally surprised. "A sojourner! How romantic! But how anybody could bear to leave Buckin'ham County is beyond me!"

"Oh, it's been twenty years since I was in Buckin'ham County, Miss Emily."

"I vow! Twenty years away from Buckin'ham County and we never knew!"

"You must be dyen to see everybody, Cousin Homer."

"Ah, yes. The absence from my dear family has been a constant ache to my heart, Miss Mamie."

Miss Emily patted the cushion beside her. "John-Boy, you just come over here and sit down. Doesn't Cousin Homer just say things in the most poetic way? He so reminds me of Ashley Longworth."

"Ashley Longworth," Cousin Homer reflected. "As I recall he was the young man your father had to shoot, wasn't he?"

"Oh, no," Miss Emily corrected, "Papa never shot him. He just shook the gun at Ashley and suggested he leave the premises."

"And he left." Miss Mamie smiled. "Like a flash."

"Ah, yes. The young man took liberties as I recall."

Miss Emily blushed. "Kissed me. Right out there under the maple tree."

"With no talk of marriage?"

"None whatsoever!" Miss Mamie said indignantly.

"Well, I'm sure he would have gotten around to a proposal sooner or later." Miss Emily smiled. "If nothen else, Ashley Longworth was a gentleman."

"No doubt. And a gentleman with superior tastes, I might add," Cousin Homer smiled.

John-Boy wondered how long their reminiscing would go on, and if the Baldwin sisters had any other work for him. The ladies didn't seem to mind, but it appeared to him that Cousin Homer overdid the compliments and sweet talk a little.

"Wouldn't it be lovely," Miss Emily sighed, "if Ashley would come back and visit again. And if we could have a grand party like we used to have when Papa was alive?"

"Why don't we just do that?" Miss Mamie said. "Why don't we just have a family reunion!"

"What a fine idea!" Miss Emily exclaimed. "A family reunion! And a big party so Cousin Homer Lee could see the whole family all at once!"

Cousin Homer looked doubtful. "Are there any Baldwins left after all these years?"

"Oh, my, yes! Why there must be hundreds of them!"

"Well, now, let me think," Miss Mamie said. "Cousin Cora moved to Washington, or some such outlandish place. And a good many of the others are dead. But never you mind, we'll round up what's left!"

"And we'll make just oceans of the Recipe!" Miss Emily said.

Cousin Homer seemed to perk up with the last statement. He emptied his goblet and smiled his approval. "Indeed, it would be a good idea to make an abundant supply of the Recipe, ladies. I must say, with due respect to the memory of your dear, departed father, I am inclined to judge that your efforts have resulted in a nectar of even superior quality."

"Oh, no," Miss Mamie protested. "We've followed Papa's Recipe precisely to the letter. We wouldn't dream of changin' it." She smiled at Miss Emily. "Perhaps Cousin Homer Lee would like a sip more."

"Ah," Cousin Homer Lee said. "A small portion, perhaps, to moisten the throat."

"You'll help us with the reunion, won't you, John-Boy?"

John-Boy hesitated, startled by the sudden question.

Helping with the reunion meant he would have to spend considerably more time at the Baldwins'.

"Of course John-Boy will help," Miss Emily said. "He has to earn enough money to pay for the new washen machine."

"Splendid!" Miss Mamie cried, "Oh, what a grand party it will be! And Emily, we're goen to have to buy more supplies. John-Boy, if we make a list, can you give it to Mr. Godsey?"

For the second time today John-Boy felt trapped. Somehow, the Baldwin sisters' enthusiasm seemed to sweep him inevitably into impossible situations. He nodded politely. "Yes'm, I can do that."

After lunch John-Boy spent the remainder of the afternoon clearing weeds from in front of the house, and then standing around while the sisters tried to figure out how furniture could be moved to provide room for a houseful of guests. Cousin Homer Lee took a nap, but he suddenly appeared from the side of the garage just as John-Boy was starting home.

"Beautiful country around here, isn't it, John-Boy," he remarked as he fell into step.

"Yes sir."

"Ah, how I envy you. A young man, springtime, the world at your doorstep. My dear cousins tell me you're the smartest boy in all Walton's Mountain."

"Well . . ." John-Boy shrugged.

"Don't be modest, son." He put an arm on John-Boy's shoulder. "The moment you stepped in that door I could see what an alert young man you are. You'll go far in this world, John-Boy. In the field of journalism you have a very high callen, and I look forward to seein' your name emblazoned in literary history alongside those of Mark Twain and my dear friend, Sinclair Lewis."

John-Boy felt a flush of embarrassment. He glanced at Cousin Homer Lee, wondering if the man really did know Sinclair Lewis.

Homer Lee frowned, his lips pursed. "Now let me see—what was it I wanted to speak to you about, John-Boy? Ah, yes, the list. I believe my dear cousins entrusted you with a list of additional supplies they might require for their forthcoming family reunion."

"Yes sir." John-Boy brought the list from his pocket.

Cousin Homer Lee stopped and gave the sheet careful study. "Ah, yes, just as I feared. Bless their dear souls, the last thing I should like to see happen to Cousin Emily and Cousin Mamie is to be accused of a lack of hospitality. As the daughters of the honorable Morley Baldwin, you can appreciate the pride they take in being gracious hostesses, can't you, John-Boy?"

"Yes sir."

"Of course you can. You are a bright boy. But in this list I foresee the possibility of a most awkward situation. You can imagine a horde of Baldwins swarming over the dear ladies' home and the unfortunate outcome of such a gathering if there should turn out to be an insufficiency of Recipe on hand for the pleasure of the guests."

"Yes sir."

Cousin Homer drew a pencil from his coat and touched it to his tongue. "Very well, John-Boy. We can insure against such a calamitous contingency by a very simple act, John-Boy, a mere stroke of the pen. Shall we say we double these figures? Twelve dozen jars instead of six dozen? And the same with grain and malt, of course. Or do you think we should triple the order?"

"Well, I—"

"No, you are quite right. Double should provide an amply comfortable margin." He handed the sheet back. "And now we can both sleep more easily, eh? You'd better hurry along, John-Boy, it'll be dark shortly."

A quarter of a mile down the road John-Boy looked back. Cousin Homer Lee was still standing on the crest of the hill. His hands were in his pockets and he seemed to be smiling. He waved, and John-Boy waved back.

John-Boy smiled to himself as he approached Ike Godsey's store. In spite of their strange behavior, Miss Emily and Miss Mamie were certainly sweet and generous old ladies. But Cousin Homer Lee was odder yet. If everyone in the Baldwin family was like the Baldwin sisters and their cousin, the upcoming reunion should be quite a sight. And twelve dozen bottles of Recipe would likely turn it into the social event of the decade.

Ike Godsey was curled over the pool table lining up a shot when John-Boy came in. Behind him, Ep Bridges, the Sheriff, was watching with a Coke in his hand.

"How you keepen, John-Boy?" Ep asked.

"Fine. Just fine."

"Been keepen on the right side of the law?"

The sheriff's narrow look made John-Boy uneasy for a minute. Helping the Baldwin sisters could probably be worked around to some kind of criminal activity if Ep Bridges wanted to make something of it.

Ep Bridges had been the Sheriff in Walton's Mountain as long as John-Boy could remember, and he was well aware of the Baldwin sisters' Recipe-making activities. But the only time he paid much attention to it was when one of the husbands of the church ladies came home a little overindulged, and the lady complained to him. On those occasions Ep drove out to the Baldwins' for a visit and then informed the aggrieved lady that it would never happen again. As long as nobody was hurt and no illegal profits were being made, Ep Bridges's philosophy was "Live and let live."

"Yes, sir," John-Boy murmured, "I been keepen on the right side of the law."

"Glad to hear it, boy. Hate to have to arrest the only writer we got in this part of the country."

Ike missed his shot. A look of disgust came to his face and he slowly straightened.

"You're tryen too hard, Ike." Ep grinned. "You gotta take it slow and easy like." He put his Coke down and studied the balls.

"Ike?" John-Boy asked. "Can I see you a minute?"

"Sure, John-Boy." Ike put down his cue and moved to the front of the store. "How'd the job work out?"

"Okay. I'd like to put a deposit on that washer. A dollar."

"Fine. I'll give you a receipt."

"You'll hold it for me now, won't you, Ike?"

Ike scribbled out a receipt. "John-Boy, if times were

better, I'd hold it till doomsday for you. But I've got to
sell that machine to the first bidder."

"But I've put a dollar down!"

"What that means is you've got nineteen to go.
Somebody else buys it, you get your dollar back."

Ike was right, he supposed. He had no real claim on
the machine until he paid up in full. He glanced over at
Sheriff Bridges, then handed Ike the note from the
Baldwin sisters. "Miss Mamie and Miss Emily want to
order some more stuff."

Ike blinked at the list. "Twelve dozen jars! You sure
they want that many?"

Ep Bridges must have heard, but he showed no sign
of it. He moved around the pool table to line up another shot.

"They're gonna have company, Ike. A big reunion
of the whole family."

"Whew," Ike breathed, "that's gonna be some reunion. Okay, John-Boy, you can tell 'em I'll have it all
in a day or two."

It had been a long day for John-Boy, but he was
pleased with himself as he started home in the
darkness. If he earned a dollar a day he would have
seven or eight dollars before school started again. And
maybe after the reunion the Baldwin sisters would still
have some work for him. Or maybe Ike would have
something by then. Between now and summertime he
could certainly find some way to earn the balance of
the twenty dollars. John-Boy turned up his collar and
smiled as he walked, picturing his mother's surprise
when he gave her the washer.

He would tell his father about it after the washer was
all paid for. Then they could drive over and pick it up
in the truck and hide it out in the barn somewhere. He
could clean it up and polish it until it looked like new
and then maybe at night, after she had gone to bed,
they could sneak it into the kitchen so she would see it
the first thing in the morning. Or maybe he could give
it to her at suppertime, when everybody was there. He
could make up a little speech about how much they all
loved her and wanted her to have something nice be-

cause they appreciated how hard she worked. And they weren't doing it because it was her birthday, or Christmas, or any other special day; she was special to them every day. John-Boy could picture her confusion and curiosity, and saying, "What in the world are you all talking about?" And then he and his father and Grandpa would go to the back door and carry it in.

The anticipation of that day gave John-Boy a rush of warmth, and redoubled his resolve to somehow get the money. He turned the corner at the old Pendleton house, and then, an instant later, all thoughts of money and washing machines fled from his mind.

It was the sound that first caught his attention—the low, almost imperceptible, vibrating notes of a pipe organ. John-Boy stopped, listening, and then once again his heart leaped into his throat as he found himself staring across the weed-covered yard of the old Pendleton house.

Was his mind playing tricks on him again? He stared, the dark silhouette of the house barely visible against the gray-black sky.

The sound came again, this time a chord—a strident, off-key dissonance in a higher register. John-Boy had no doubts now. The sounds were from an organ and they were coming from inside the house. The notes held for a moment, then went silent again.

John-Boy's heart pounded. He didn't believe in ghosts. Nor did he believe an organ could play by itself. For a full minute he stared at the dark shutters, scarcely breathing, waiting, listening intently for the sounds to resume. But now there was only silence.

Had he been seen? Was someone at the window now, peering out at him from the darkened house? John-Boy's gaze moved slowly across the shuttered windows of the lower floor, and then to the exposed window above. For another half minute he stared at it, the pale reflection gazing mutely back at him.

John-Boy slowly licked his dry lips. He glanced over the dark house again, then turned quickly and hurried away.

A hundred yards up the road he glanced backward without slackening his pace. There was no one in sight. The house looked cold and lonely and deserted now.

III

"You sure you weren't haven hallucinations, John-Boy?"

"I heard it, Daddy. There's somebody in that house. And last night when I was comen home I saw a light in one of the upstairs windows. I just saw it for a minute, and I wasn't too sure, but I know somebody was playen the organ there tonight."

Grandpa was chuckling, but everyone else at the table was listening in wide-eyed silence.

"Well," John said, "I guess we'd better have a look. Dave Pendleton gave me a key and I promised to keep an eye on the place."

"I'm scared," Elizabeth breathed.

"You finish your supper first, John-Boy," Olivia said. John-Boy had started his story as soon as he sat down at the table, but he still hadn't taken a bite.

"That's right," Grandpa laughed. "The worst thing you can do is go after ghosts on an empty stomach."

"Oh, hush, old man," Grandma said. "What do you know about chasen ghosts?"

29

"Daddy," John-Boy said with an uneasy laugh, "if there's a ghost there, I don't promise but what my feet might run off with me."

John nodded. "If there's a ghost there, my feet will be travelin' right along besides yours, son."

After supper John got his hunting rifle and the whole family watched while he lighted the kerosene lantern and the two of them pulled on their jackets.

"Maybe you ought to get Ep Bridges to go along with you," Olivia suggested.

"I think Grandpa ought to go," Erin suggested slyly. "He's not afraid of ghosts."

John shook his head. "No, sweetheart, Grandpa might scare 'em all to death."

Grandpa grinned, and they left with Olivia cautioning them to be careful.

The lantern in his father's hand cast a swinging cone of yellow light that turned the surrounding darkness into an impenetrable black void. From their house the rutted dirt road curved downward and skirted along a row of tall spruce trees until it branched off toward the Pendletons'. In spite of his certainty that there were no such things as ghosts, and that whatever it was inside that house must be explainable in human terms, John-Boy still felt the dryness steadily growing in his throat.

"What do you think it might be, Daddy?"

"Don't know, John-Boy. Lots of people wanderen around these days with no jobs and no place to stay."

His father let it go at that, and John-Boy envisioned a group of hungry hobos lounging in the Pendleton house. Was the light he had seen the flickering of a campfire they had built in one of the upper bedrooms? Or maybe there was only one man—a fugitive hiding out from the law? That thought sent John-Boy's heart ripping a couple beats faster.

"Hold it, John-Boy."

His father's voice was hushed and he stopped walking, his head cocked to the side.

John-Boy paused. Then he heard it too—the distant, eerie chords of an organ.

"That's it, Daddy. That's what I heard earlier."

"Well, I'll be damned!"

They were less than a hundred yards from the house, but no lights were visible. The dark silhouette was only a ghostly shadow against the chilly night sky.

"Okay, let's just take it easy," his father said. He shifted his rifle and moved forward again.

The organ music grew more powerful as they approached, as if building to some kind of dramatic climax. John-Boy swallowed hard and stuck close to his father's elbow as he pushed open the gate and moved cautiously to the front steps.

"Daddy?"

"Umm?"

"Maybe we should get the Sheriff, like Mama said."

His father set the lantern down and got out his keys. "Well," he said softly, "I think I'd just as soon get it over with right now. What do you think?"

John-Boy nodded, not trusting his voice. Then he held his breath as his father turned the key and slowly eased the door open.

The entry hall was empty except for a single straight-backed chair and an umbrella holder that stood near the base of the staircase. Everything was thick and gray with dust. The music seemed to be coming from the open double doors on the left. John looked the place over, then lifted the lantern and moved to the doors. He stopped abruptly, the exclamation choking in his throat.

"Well, I'll be damned!"

There are no such things as ghosts. John-Boy had silently repeated this fact a dozen times on their way to the house. And yet he was fully prepared to see a swirl of transparent vapor hovering over the bench in front of the organ. What he saw startled him even more. It was a girl—a young girl with long black tresses reaching almost to her waist.

For an instant they all stared at each other. The girl's hands leaped from the organ keys as she twisted and gaped fearfully at them. And then she was gone. With three quick steps she was at the shuttered doors leading to the back, and in what seemed like one movement she swung one of them open and disappeared.

"Little girl!" John called, but the only response was the banging of a screen door that led to the backyard. John-Boy and his father hurried to the porch and then out the back door. "There's no need to be scared!" John shouted. "Wait!"

The yard was almost pitch black. But then, from the light of his father's lifted lantern, John-Boy caught a glimpse of the girl's skirt disappearing into a latticed summerhouse. "In there, Daddy!" They strode to within a few feet of the entrance and stopped.

"Young lady," John called. "My name is John Walton, and this boy's my son."

They stood silently for a minute, but there was no answer.

"We didn't mean to scare you that way. John-Boy saw lights over here, and I promised Dave Pendleton I'd keep an eye on this place."

For another half minute there was no sound. Then some dry leaves rustled and the girl moved hesitantly into sight. She was about sixteen, John-Boy guessed. Her silky black hair was parted in the middle, half of it now tumbling down the left side of her blouse. He was amazed at how pretty she was, and how frightened she looked gazing out at them.

"Don't be afraid now," John said. "What're you doen here, miss?"

She studied them for a minute, and then, as if apologizing, said, "Dave Pendleton is my father."

"Jenny? You're Jenny Pendleton? Dave Pendleton's little girl?"

"Yes."

"Jenny Pendleton!" John-Boy's father laughed in disbelief. "Why, last time I saw you, you were just a baby! By golly! But that was a long time ago, wasn't it."

She nodded and gave John-Boy a sheepish glance. "Mr. Walton, it was very nice of you to check up on things here, but I'm all right. You don't have to worry about me."

"Are you all alone here?"

"Yes, but I'm fine. Really I am. Dave and Eula will

probably come in a few days and I'll just wait till they're here."

"Who's Eula?"

"My father's married again."

"Oh, I see." John-Boy's father nodded thoughtfully. "Jenny, I want you to get your things together and come over and spend the night with us. I've got a little girl of my own near your age, and I sure wouldn't want her out here by herself."

"I don't want to be any trouble." It was a weak protest, suggesting she had had enough of this spooky old house.

John-Boy smiled at her. "Come on. I'll help you get your things."

Everyone was in pajamas by the time they got home. But none of them had any intention of going to bed until the mystery was solved. John and John-Boy brought Jenny Pendleton into a kitchen full of gaping, awestruck faces.

"Here's your ghost," John said, "Miss Jennifer Pendleton, lately of St. Petersburg, Florida."

After a moment of stunned silence, the questions came like a crashing avalanche. No, her parents were not with her; they would be in Walton's Mountain very soon. She had ridden a bus all alone from St. Petersburg to Savannah, and then to Richmond where she hitched a ride to Walton's Mountain. Yes, she had stayed in that spooky house all by herself last night and all day today. Yes, she was a little hungry.

And with that revelation Olivia shooed everyone out of the kitchen and up to bed so the girl could eat in peace.

When the others were gone, Olivia warmed up some leftover meat and potatoes, but she didn't ask the girl any more questions. She was curious enough, wondering why Jenny was in Walton's Mountain all by herself, and whether or not Dave Pendleton knew where she was. But if any confessions were to be made, Olivia felt it was better for them to come out voluntarily.

But apparently Jenny was not ready to unburden herself. While she ate she asked about the Walton family and seemed content to let Olivia do most of the talking.

For Mary Ellen, Erin, and Elizabeth, the girl's adventures riding around the country and spending a night in that house were far more intriguing than was the question of why she wasn't with her parents. When Olivia brought Jenny up to their room and a place was arranged for her to sleep, a new barrage of questions came, this time asked with hushed admiration. Weren't you scared traveling all by yourself? What did you do in that spooky house all day? Is it haunted? What did you eat? And then Erin shifted her questions and got what seemed like the oddest answer of all. "Don't you have any brothers or sisters?" she asked.

"No," Jenny told them, "I'm an only child."

This revelation was as startling and bizarre to the three Walton girls as was Jenny's experience of being in a household teeming with other children.

Elizabeth found the idea of being an only child incomprehensible. "But why didn't you get some brothers and sisters?"

The three older girls laughed. "Elizabeth, did you know that you are a very pretty girl?" Jenny said.

The evasion was successful. Elizabeth stared at her for a minute, then shook her head. "I don't think I'm as pretty as you are. You have the prettiest hair I've ever seen. But I've got a tadpole named after me."

"You do? Will you show it to me tomorrow?"

Mary Ellen reached under her bed and came up with the gallon jar. "You can see it right now if you want."

"Ecchh!" Erin cried and pulled her feet off the floor. "You're not supposed to have that in here!"

"You want one named after you?" Elizabeth asked.

"Yes, I do." Jenny frowned thoughtfully at the jar, then pointed. "That one."

Elizabeth jumped from her bed and looked closely at the jar. "Which one?"

"That one."

"Oh." Elizabeth frowned uncertainly at the slithering mass of polliwogs and finally smiled. "Hello, Jenny," she said.

"Good night, Elizabeth. Good night, Erin. Good night, Mary Ellen. Good night, Jenny."

It was Jason's voice coming from the next room. Then came Jim-Bob's and John-Boy's voices, followed by those of all the others in the family.

Jenny listened, amazed at first, and then delighted by the never-ending chorus. When they were finished she returned the calls, with Mary Ellen whispering to her the names of those she couldn't remember.

"Do you do that every night?" she whispered when the house was finally silent.

"Do what?"

"Say good night that way?"

"Sure."

"That's wonderful."

"It is unless there's a bunch of relatives here," Erin smiled. "Then it's practically mornen before everybody gets said good night to."

Jenny laughed. The other girls were now snuggled under the covers, and she eased down from her elbow and pulled the thick comforter up to her chin. She had never seen a family quite like this one. And yet she knew, somehow, that this was the kind of family she had always wanted. And that was at least part of the reason she had run away. She closed her eyes and smiled, trying to remember all the names again. But she was asleep before she got past three or four of them.

After the good-nights, John-Boy sat at his desk for another ten minutes, gazing idly at the blank notebook in front of him. He wasn't certain what he wanted to write down. He wasn't even certain of what he thought about Jenny Pendleton. There was no question of her being about the prettiest girl he had ever laid eyes on. He had been struck by this fact the minute he saw her standing out in that backyard with the lantern light on her face. And then, after they got home, he had caught himself staring at her in the kitchen. And when she looked back at him he felt a crazy kind of embarrassment he had never experienced before. With no change of expression her eyes seemed to smile as if they were softly saying that she liked him. It was a brand-new experience for John-Boy.

But to write something like that down on paper would be crazy, he guessed. It would all look pretty silly if someone happened to read it.

John-Boy finally brought his attention back to the blank pad. He drew it closer and slowly wrote the name *Jenny* on the top line. That would be enough, he figured. It was an important day in his life, and he wouldn't forget what that single entry meant. He finally returned the pad to the desk drawer, climbed into bed, and switched off the lamp.

He could hear no sounds from the girls' room. He listened for a minute and then smiled, picturing Jenny's hair spread across the pillow as she slept. He hoped she liked it here.

The familiar early-morning sounds drifted softly into John-Boy's consciousness. From his parents' bedroom the muffled ring of the alarm clock was stopped abruptly. A minute later the bedsprings creaked, there was the shuffling of feet, and he knew his father was pulling on his faded overalls. The heavy footsteps clamored down the stairs, followed by the clunking of kerosene-soaked wood being tossed into the stove. Then the screen door slapped gently shut and John-Boy knew his father was crossing the yard toward the barn, his hands in his jacket pockets and his shoulders hunched against the predawn chill. Ten minutes later his return was signaled by another slap of the screen door and the clunk of the full milk pail on the kitchen table.

By this time his mother was already dressed and going down the stairs. There was a soft murmur of conversation and then the faint aroma of perking coffee was followed by the growing sizzle of cooking bacon.

It was going to be a warm day. Through his window John-Boy could see the first rays of sunlight already touching the peak of Walton's Mountain. He closed his eyes for a minute, smiling, thinking about the day ahead. It was Sunday. There would be no rush to awaken everybody. And after breakfast they would all be going to church.

He wondered if Jenny Pendleton went to church in St. Petersburg. He could imagine how pretty she would look in a long white dress and her black hair tumbling down from a big picture hat. And she would have flowers in her hand. John-Boy held the picture in his mind for several minutes, seeing her in a front pew of the church, singing, then standing on the church steps, the sun filtering through her bonnet. Then he was walking home with her, both of them talking, laughing happily over some story. And then, after lunch—

John-Boy's early-morning daydreams evaporated with an abrupt and sobering thought. He had forgotten something. In all the excitement over chasing ghosts and bringing Jenny Pendleton home last night, no one had questioned him about where he had been all day yesterday. Even he had forgotten about his job with the Baldwin sisters. John-Boy drew in his breath at the recollection, and his promise to go back out there today. It would have been difficult enough telling his mother about it last night. But today, on the Sabbath, with her thoughts on church and God's wrathful attitude toward the sinful activities of the Baldwin sisters—it would be hopeless.

Still, he had to do it. It would be impossible to slip away unnoticed for another afternoon. And such deception would lead to certain disaster.

For several minutes John-Boy gazed at the ceiling, reflecting on his predicament. Then, grateful for the interruption, he slid from under the covers and looked out to see what Reckless was barking at.

It was Sheriff Ep Bridges. John-Boy watched as Ep brought his old Ford to a rattling halt in front of the house. As he climbed out, Reckless's frenzied yelps turned to tail-wagging and they both disappeared around the side, headed for the back door. It was a strange time for the sheriff to come calling. John-Boy dressed as quickly as he could. Was it something to do with Jenny?

"Mornen, John-Boy." Ep smiled when John-Boy came into the kitchen. The Sheriff was seated at the table, a cup of steaming coffee already in his hand. From the cheerful manner of the other greetings it didn't look like he had brought any bad news—or at least he hadn't announced it yet.

"Eggs, John-Boy? And how 'bout you, Sheriff? We've got plenty."

"No, thanks, Livvy. Ate 'bout an hour ago. Coffee's fine."

John Walton had already finished his eggs. He took his dirty plate to the sink. "What're you doen up so early, John-Boy? Didn't you sleep good last night?"

"I slept fine, Daddy. Just felt like getten up."

All the social amenities seemed to be taken care of, and there was a pause, everyone waiting for Sheriff Bridges to explain the purpose of his visit. He took a sip of coffee and frowned.

"I'm really sorry to barge in here at this time of day. 'Specially on Sunday. But late last night I had a call from Dave Pendleton in Richmond. Seems that little girl of his has run away."

"That so?" John said.

Ep nodded. "Dave seems to think she might have come here to Walton's Mountain. You haven't seen nothen of her, have you?"

John grinned. "Not since about eleven last night. She's fine, Ep. Jenny's here, sleepin' upstairs with the girls right now."

"That a fact? Well, I'm relieved to hear that. She's okay, huh?"

"Seems to be. I guess she's been around here since Thursday night. Spent one night at the old Pendleton place, then John-Boy here heard her playen the organ last night and me and him went over and brought her home."

Ep nodded. "Well, seems Dave's got himself married again, and he kind of intimated Jenny didn't take a shine to the idea." He finished his coffee and rose. "I hate to run off, but I better get to a telephone and let Dave know where she is. Meantime, I'd appreciate it if you'd keep an eye on her."

"We'll do our best, Sheriff. Don't worry about it."

"Okay, thanks for the coffee, Livvy."

After the door closed, John-Boy picked at his eggs, wondering what Jenny's running away would mean. If she didn't like her stepmother, would she have to go back and live with her anyway?

"Too bad," John said. "That happens sometimes, I expect."

Olivia shook her head. "And on top of all the other troubles Dave's had."

"Will he come and get her?" John-Boy asked.

"I reckon." His father looked thoughtful for a minute, then looked past John-Boy and smiled. "Well, speak of the angel, look who's up already. Mornen, Jenny."

With her hair neatly brushed, and smiling cheerfully, Jenny looked as fresh as a spring flower this morning. "Good morning, everybody."

"How'd you sleep, young lady?"

"Very well, thank you."

"How would you like your eggs, Jenny? Scrambled?"

"Scrambled is fine, thank you. I'm not taking anybody's place, am I?" She paused at the chair across from John-Boy, giving him a questioning smile.

"Room for everybody." John laughed. "At least for an hour or so."

For some crazy reason John-Boy felt tongue-tied, as if Jenny's glowing presence rendered speech impossible. Her gentle smile as she sat down seemed to aggravate the problem even more.

"I hope you'll be goen to church with us this mornen," Olivia said. "It looks like it's goen to be a beautiful day."

"Oh, I'd love to."

"I'm sure Mary Ellen must have an extra dress and hat if you don't have one with you."

"No, I don't. That would be wonderful. And Mrs. Walton, I . . . I think it's awfully nice of you to take me in like this. And I want to help. I'd love to do the dishes for you after breakfast. And I can sweep and dust, or clean windows, or anything you'd like me to do."

"I could use another hand in the sawmill." John smiled.

"Oh, I'll be glad to help if I can."

"Now, now," Olivia said, delivering her eggs, "you won't be workin' in any sawmill around here. John is just haven fun. We'll find somethin' to keep you busy."

"Well, John-Boy," his father sighed, "I guess we'll just have to saw up those logs all by ourselves. We might as well get started." He downed the last of his coffee, but hesitated as an anxious look came to Jenny's face. "What's the matter, Jenny?"

"Nothing," she said quickly. "In fact, I guess it's just the opposite."

Olivia frowned. "I don't understand, Jenny."

"There's nothing to understand, really. I mean it's just that ... well ..." She took a deep breath and smiled hopefully. "Mr. and Mrs. Walton, is there any chance ... I mean, do you ever take in boarders at your house?"

The question startled all of them. John and Olivia exchanged a glance, and John-Boy's heart leaped for a moment at the thought of Jenny boarding with them. But then he remembered the Sheriff's visit.

Olivia smiled. "Well, we don't take in boarders on a regular basis."

"I was wondering," Jenny said, "if maybe you would take me in for a while. I'd pay and I wouldn't be any trouble."

"I'm sure you wouldn't be any trouble at all, Jenny. But you're welcome to stay as long as you like. And we couldn't take any money for it."

Jenny smiled, but then bit her lip. "There's something I have to tell you, though. Dad doesn't know I'm here."

John smiled, relieved by her confession. "I reckon he knows by now, Jenny. The Sheriff was here before you got up this mornen. Your father called him last night."

The news didn't seem to surprise Jenny. She nodded as if accepting her fate.

"Jenny?" Olivia asked. "Why did you run away?"

"I didn't really run away," she murmured. "Dad and Eula were off on their honeymoon, so I just decided I'd make a trip to Walton's Mountain. I've wanted to come here ever since I found some letters of my mother's. She loved it here."

John-Boy felt a lump in his chest, and had an urge to reach across and take her hand, or say something comforting. But Jenny quickly brightened, dropping the matter.

"If I'm going to be one of the family, I'd better hurry up and get to work, hadn't I."

"What you'd better do," Olivia smiled, "is eat your breakfast before it all gets cold."

John studied Jenny for a minute, then pushed his chair back. "Come on, John-Boy. You and me are the ones who better get to work."

John Walton smiled to himself as he and John-Boy went out the back door. In all his life he could not remember John-Boy sitting through an entire breakfast without saying a single word. But he guessed there were some pretty strong palpitations inside the boy's ribs. The first stirrings of love were powerful medicine. And he certainly couldn't blame him. Dave Pendleton's little girl had blossomed into a mighty handsome young lady.

"Let's get them logs off the truck first, John-Boy."

John-Boy nodded and headed for the truck, his thoughts apparently miles away.

"John-Boy, I'd certainly admire to hear that nice voice of yours sometime before the day is over."

It took a minute for the statement to penetrate. Then John-Boy grinned. "Okay, Daddy."

IV

John Walton sometimes wondered if he wasn't crazy to keep on cutting wood for a living. The crazy part of it was that the living it produced was so close to nothing that it hardly seemed worth the effort. The commercial sawmill down in Charlottesville had bigger trucks for hauling logs, they had giant saws for cutting them, and power hoists to swing the logs into the saws and to load the finished lumber. The number of two-by-fours or finished boards John could produce in a twelve-hour day, they could turn out in ten minutes. So the price he got when he hauled them down to the retail lumberyard or sold them to his neighbors was determined by the prices being charged in Charlottesville.

"That's nice, seasoned lumber, John," he was usually told, "but they're chargen only eight cents a board in Charlottesville. Reckon I can give you nine to save me a trip down there."

From a seven-day workweek such prices brought only enough to buy the feed and gasoline and flour and sugar to keep them all alive and working from day to day. What little might be left over was used for thread and sewing materials to keep them warm. If there were ever two or three dollars left over after that, John felt like some kind of miracle had happened.

At times it all seemed hopeless. As often as he had told himself that next year would be better, the next year turned out to be the same. If the winter was mild, he could cut far more firewood, but the need for it dwindled. In a cold winter like the one they just had, the struggle to cut and deliver it was too time-consuming and it was impossible to realize any profit. And there were so few people in a position to pay cash, most of the money he collected went into gasoline for the truck and the saw motor. So the endless, slow-moving merry-go-round went on with each summer and winter promising nothing better than before.

At other times John felt he was lucky. He had been to Charlottesville, and last year he had taken a trip to Richmond, and in both places he had seen men standing in line waiting for a bowl of soup, while others went from door to door, or stood hopelessly on street corners, or hopped freights, all hoping desperately that someone would give them a day's work, or maybe a half day's work, or that some other town might prove more promising than this one. Most of these men must have had families, and John couldn't help wondering if their wives and children had anything at all to eat, or if they had clothing or beds to sleep on. Coming home from those trips John couldn't help but count his blessings. But he often wondered what it was all coming to.

At least the Walton family was surviving, and they were together. If the hogs or the cow didn't get sick, and the bugs or the frost or the summer thundershowers didn't wipe out the vegetable garden, and if he could earn enough money to buy the other necessities, they could carry on another year, and maybe another year after that, and maybe by then things might get better.

The subject of economics was a pure mystery to John Walton. So many people needed food and houses and clothing, and there were so many people without jobs who knew how to build houses and grow food and make clothing, it didn't make much sense that something couldn't be done. Now there was even talk of having farmers plow under their crops and kill off their livestock. How such a thing would help feed hungry people was beyond him.

The only politician he had ever seen in his life was a man named Colin Pierce, who was a congressman and gave a speech a few years back in Charlottesville. But from the look of the man's hands, John doubted if he knew which end of a cow the milk came out of. All he talked about was how terrible Herbert Hoover had been, and how, if Colin Pierce was reelected, things would get a lot better. Herbert Hoover had been gone a good number of years now, and Colin Pierce had been reelected three times to the Congress. But things were pretty much the same, and John Walton no longer put much store in politicians.

He was thinking about these things, maneuvering a heavy log into position in front of the whirling saw, when John-Boy made his startling announcement.

"I'm gonna buy Mama a washen machine, Daddy."

John-Boy was guiding the far end of the log, bringing it around into a straight line with the saw, and from the casual tone of his voice he might have been commenting on the weather.

"You're goen to do *what?*" John asked.

"A washen machine. Ike Godsey's got a used one down at the store. He told me I could have it for only twenty dollars."

John stared incredulously at the boy for a minute, then turned his attention back to the log. "Okay, push her through."

John-Boy pushed and John guided while the blade screamed through the twelve-foot length. It was a good cut. They each picked up one of the halves and carried it back for a second cut.

"Twenty dollars is a whole lot of money, John-Boy."

"I got a job, Daddy. I've already paid Ike a dollar."

"That where you were all day yesterday?"

"Yes. And I gotta do some more work this afternoon."

They ran one of the split pieces through again, John guiding it more carefully this time, making a neat two-inch-thick plank. He couldn't help but be pleased by the boy's good intentions. But twenty dollars! That was a whole lot of money.

"Where you worken?"

"Well, that's somethen I wanted to talk to you about, Daddy. I'm worken for the Baldwin sisters."

"The Baldwin sisters!"

"Yes, sir."

John-Boy was full of surprises today. "You helpen 'em make that Recipe?"

"No, nothen like that. I'm just helpen 'em clean up around the place. Their cousin Homer Lee from Buckin'ham County is visitin' and they're plannen a big family reunion."

"I see. You told your mama about this?"

"No. Not yet."

John grunted and reset the saw guides to trim the planks. As long as John-Boy wasn't learning the fine art of whiskey manufacturing, he saw no harm in his working for the Baldwins. But there was no doubt Olivia wouldn't look at it quite that way.

"You want me to help with your mama?"

"I'd sure appreciate it, Daddy."

John smiled. "Well, it's for a good cause. I don't see no reason to upset your mama by tellen her about it, do you? At least not if she don't ask." He glanced past John-Boy. "Mornen, Grandpa."

Grandpa Walton looked like he had consumed a very satisfying breakfast as he surveyed their production. "This all you boys got done this mornen. Guess you'd better let me take over, John-Boy."

Grandpa Walton worked harder on Sunday than on any other day of the week. His diligence on the day of rest provided a good excuse for him not to go to church. John-Boy smiled and stepped aside. "There's another favor I'd like to ask you, Daddy."

"What's that?"

"I have to deliver some things to the Baldwins' this afternoon. I wonder if I could use the truck."

"Well, I don't know, son. You go streaken around in

that truck without a driven permit, Sheriff's gonna pick you up for sure."

"It's not far, Daddy."

"It's not the distance, son, it's—"

"I'll go with the boy, John," Grandpa offered. "If anybody stops us, they'll have to deal with me!"

John regarded the old man with a half smile. "Grandpa, you want them ladies to have their supplies? Or you just interested in a sip of their Recipe?"

Grandpa considered the question, then grinned. "Never told a lie in my life. So I'd have to say the answer to that is *both.*"

"John-Boy, looks like you've got yourself the truck."

"Jenny's goen to live with us," Elizabeth announced when John-Boy returned to the house. "She's goen to help us collect polliwogs, and she's goen to earn six million dollars, too."

Everyone was up and almost finished with breakfast now, and Jenny was already working hard at the dishes.

"We're goen to *share* the six million dollars," Jim-Bob corrected.

"Isn't that wonderful, John-Boy?" Mary Ellen asked.

"Yes, it is."

John-Boy glanced at Jenny, but she didn't look up from the sink. As he went up the stairs he heard his mother cautioning everyone not to get dirty before they went to church. Her refusal to let them collect more tadpoles this morning brought a chorus of protests.

In his room, John-Boy got out his pad again and gazed thoughtfully at the single word *Jenny* written at the top of the page.

Jenny Pendleton was not going to live with them. As soon as her father came she would be taken to Richmond, or back to Florida, and John-Boy doubted if he would ever see her again. Then the passage of time would quickly erase the memory of her, and the entry of her name in his notebook would be nothing more than a curious footnote in his past. John-Boy turned the page and sat back, deliberately shifting his thoughts to the Baldwin sisters.

He could understand his mother's distaste for their Recipe-making activities. And John-Boy had heard stories around Walton's Mountain that the two ladies occasionally accepted gifts from callers and returned such generosity with mason jars full of Recipe. But if it were ever suggested that these exchanges were commercial transactions, he imagined the two sisters would be horrified. A number of years ago during Prohibition, John-Boy had heard, the stream of callers bearing gifts for the Baldwin sisters was almost endless.

John-Boy smiled as he made notes describing the musty elegance of the Baldwin house. If, instead of the Recipe, the two ladies were famous for their canned peaches or strawberry preserves, he suspected his mother would be their most sympathetic customer and greatest admirer. She would be forever marveling on how those wonderful sisters were able to make ends meet and still conduct themselves with such dignity.

He wrote:

The Baldwin sisters were like the old clock in their parlor that no longer ticked. They had chosen their favorite time, they were happy in it, and had no desire to move on.

"Boo!"

John-Boy was so absorbed in writing he had heard no one enter his room. He lifted his head with a start, then quickly smiled.

It was Jenny. She had come only halfway through the door and was regarding him with a questioning smile, a feather duster in her hand.

"Don't let me interrupt."

"You're not interrupten. Come on in."

"I'm dusting." She moved to the dresser and brushed it lightly. "I've finished the dishes and fed Reckless, so now I'm helping your mother clean house."

John-Boy smiled. His mother always gave the house a thorough cleaning on Saturday, reserving Sunday for church and cooking meals. It was interesting that of all the rooms in the house Jenny apparently had chosen his to dust first.

"What's that on your head?" John-Boy asked. She was wearing what looked like a nineteenth-century bonnet.

"Your grandmother gave it to me. She said in the olden days the women of the house used to wear them while they did the chores. How do I look?"

"Not exactly like a pioneer lady." To himself, John-Boy thought she looked beautiful. He felt a flush of embarrassment as she rose on her toes for a minute, revealing the backs of her knees. She had beautifully smooth legs, and she moved like a dancer.

"Well, I *feel* like a pioneer lady. I feel like a pioneer mother struggling to raise a family in the wilderness." She turned sharply. "Shouldn't you be out milking the cow or chopping wood or something?"

"I already chopped wood."

She frowned at the note pad on his desk. "What are you writing there, anyway?"

"Oh . . . just stuff."

"Have you written anything in there about me?"

"Well . . . yes."

"What did you say?"

"I'm not going to tell you."

She gazed narrowly at him for a minute and then brushed the feather duster lightly across the front of the dresser. "What do you think of me?"

"I don't know *what* to make of you."

"I know a lot about you."

"Like what?"

She smiled. "I've been talking to your mother. She told me about your wanting to be a writer."

John-Boy couldn't tell if she approved or disapproved. She moved around the room, swishing at nonexistent dust.

"I want to," he said. "What about you?"

She seemed to be waiting for the question. She sat down on the bed and sighed dreamily. "More than anything else in the world, I'd like to belong to this family."

Again John-Boy was startled by her statement. He shrugged. "You do belong. You're here. Everybody likes you."

"Do you?"

The directness of the question took him off guard. "Well . . . sure."

She stared at him, her eyes sparkling, then looked quickly into the corner. "What's that?"

John-Boy looked, relieved by the change of subject. "Haven't you ever seen a dulcimer before?"

"I've heard of them. Where did you get it?"

"There's a man down the road—old Mr. Dawson—who makes them. I never could afford one, but once in a while he lets me bring one home to play."

"What does it sound like?"

John-Boy hesitated, wondering if she really wanted to hear it, or if she was just making conversation. He suddenly felt awkward as she watched him cross the room and bring the instrument back to the chair. Without looking at her he strummed it softly. Then, in a hushed voice, he sang:

> Little birdie, little birdie,
> Come and sing me your song,
> I've a short time to be with you,
> And a long time to be gone.

When he looked up she was smiling, her chin cupped in her hands. "Is there more?"

John-Boy strummed again.

> Little birdie, little birdie,
> What makes you fly so high?
> You must have another to love
> Way up in the blue sky.

John-Boy had no idea what it was like to be in love. But when he finished the song and looked at her, it was as if he and Jenny had known each other all their lives. For what seemed like a full minute he gazed into her deep brown eyes and she gazed back, and neither of them moved nor breathed. In that long moment the outside world did not exist. Her father was not coming to take her home, all time stood still, and Jenny Pendleton and John-Boy Walton were telling each other every guarded secret of their lives.

It was Jenny who finally broke away. As if her throat were suddenly dry, she turned quickly to the side and swallowed hard. Then, as abruptly, she came to her feet and looked out the window. "Why do they call it Walton's Mountain?"

John-Boy set the dulcimer aside. Once again he was conscious of voices and laughter downstairs, and his father's saw began a long, lengthwise screech through a log.

"It was named after my great-grandpa."

"Oh? Does your family still own the mountain?"

She was staring intently out the window, but her voice was strained. John-Boy cleared his own throat. "Only the top of it and one side. My uncles sold their parts."

"I'd love to go up there sometime."

John-Boy rose, but something constrained him from going near her. He took the dulcimer back to the corner. "My daddy wants to build a house up there some day. I can take you up and see the spot. I could do it tomorrow morning if you want."

She turned, her smile controlled. "I'd really like to, John-Boy." It was as if both of them had reached some dizzying height and were now carefully trying to work their way down.

"I'd enjoy it too. The chimney from my great-grandpa's house is still up there. The house burned down a long time ago."

She laughed nervously and picked up the feather duster. "I really haven't gotten any dusting done at all. And now I guess I'd better get ready for church."

"Me too."

It seemed crazy, but neither of them knew what to say for a minute. Jenny was going only as far as the next bedroom, and yet both of them felt the need to say something about the separation. Too much had happened to ignore it. But saying good-bye seemed to give the event too much explicit recognition.

"I guess you're goin' to wear one of Mary Ellen's hats," John-Boy finally said.

"Yes."

"I think it'll look good on you."

It was a ridiculous statement and both of them knew it. He had no idea which hat she would be wearing. Jenny smiled, trying to hold back a giggle, and John-Boy laughed.

"Well, whatever hat it is, it'll look good," he said, "At least a lot better than the one you have on."

"Well," she said with sudden mock indignance, "if that's the way you feel, John-Boy Walton, I am leaving this room right this minute!" She lifted her head and marched out.

There was a magnificent formation of cumulus clouds piled up to the north. But they seemed to be stationary, and overhead the sun was shining with unusual warmth and brilliance.

John-Boy held Elizabeth's hand as they all walked down the road to church. He had never enjoyed a Sunday morning walk to church quite so much.

Jason, Ben, and Jim-Bob had gone on ahead, and were throwing rocks at trees and fence posts and tin cans, while the others followed in a more decorous group. Olivia, Grandma, Jenny, and Mary Ellen walked in front, and John-Boy, Elizabeth, and Erin brought up the rear.

Jenny's floppy hat was yellow and had a broad orange ribbon that was almost a perfect match for the small flowers on her white dress. She too seemed to be enjoying the walk, and occasionally turned with a bright smile for Elizabeth and John-Boy behind her.

Once they were within sight of the church they met other members of the congregation. They exchanged favorable comments about the weather, some expressed regrets about not seeing John and Grandpa coming to the services on such a lovely day, and then they all filed inside and sat down in respectful silence.

It seemed to John-Boy that his voice had an extraordinary richness this morning, and he sang out the hymns with vibrant joy. "Bringing in the Sheaves" and "Rock of Ages" resounded from the church and echoed across the valley with uninhibited conviction.

Reverend Bascombe's sermon dealt with the house that "fell not; for it was founded on a rock," and he warned all sinners of the perilous road ahead if they did not mend their ways.

Coming out of the church and into the sunshine, Jenny paused briefly on the steps, and was even more beautiful than John-Boy had imagined she would be. She was the center of attention, everyone inquiring about life in Florida and her father's new bride.

When they finally started home there was the same grouping, and the three younger boys were quickly out of sight as they raced home. Elizabeth asked questions about the minister's sermon, and while Erin answered them, John-Boy kept his eyes on Jenny, watching her every step and gesture and the tilt of her head as she questioned Olivia and Grandma about the people she had met at the church. He could imagine no actress or beauty queen or movie star being more beautiful than Jenny Pendleton. The thick tassel of black hair below her hat glistened in the sunshine, and each time she smiled at Grandma or Olivia on either side of her, a shiver of joy ran through John-Boy's spine.

And then, as they finally came within sight of the house, John-Boy saw the sudden stiffness come into her back.

"Looks like we've got visitors," Grandma remarked.

"With a new car," Olivia added. "Who do you suppose it could be?"

Jenny supplied the answer, her voice hardly a murmur. "It's Dad and Eula," she said, and John-Boy's heart sank.

The arrival of Dave and Eula Pendleton was certainly no great surprise. But through the last two-and-a-half hours, since the moment Jenny came into his room with the feather duster, John-Boy had conveniently ignored the fact. Now, grimly, he realized how foolish he had been. Jenny gave him a brief, apprehensive glance, and they all filed into the house.

"Look who's here, everybody!" John Walton grinned, "Dave and Eula Pendleton! Dave and Eula, this is the rest of the family. That's Elizabeth there with the pretty dress. This is . . ."

Jenny's new stepmother was seated on the sofa, a cup and saucer in her hand. She was a pleasant-looking woman, in her early forties, John-Boy guessed. By the standards of Walton's Mountain she was dressed elegantly—more like women in the city—in a gray suit and white blouse and silk stockings. Her hair was slightly reddish and she smiled warmly at each of the Waltons as they were introduced. At the end her eyes went back to Jenny and the smile softened.

Dave Pendleton stood by the fireplace, also wearing a suit. He was a prosperous-looking man and there seemed to be great love in his eyes as he gazed at his daughter.

"And this young lady," John finally laughed, referring to Jenny, "I reckon you're already acquainted with her."

Jenny had stopped just inside the room, tense, as if ready for the worst. "You pretty mad with me, Dad?"

Dave Pendleton slowly shook his head, his smile leaving no doubt about his feelings. "Jenny, you're too old to spank and too young to send to jail. What am I going to do with you?"

Jenny looked like she was going to burst into happy tears. "You could give me a kiss," she said, and hurried across to his suddenly outstretched arms.

John-Boy felt a little relieved as they hugged each other. No matter how bad things might have been for Jenny, it looked like she and her father loved each other very much. Mrs. Pendleton was also smiling happily, and Jenny kissed her cheek with what looked like genuine affection.

"Sorry I worried you, Eula, I really am."

"You're forgiven, sweetheart. We're just happy to see you're in such good hands."

"Well," Dave Pendleton said, "I think it was more our fault than it was yours, Jenny. We just got so busy preparing for the wedding and everything, I guess you got the feeling we didn't even know you were around. But we're gonna make up for that."

Jenny sat down next to Eula. "I really thought your honeymoon would be more fun without me hanging around."

John laughed out loud and Olivia flushed. "Have you all eaten?" she asked quickly. "We can easily set two more places at the table."

"No, no, we don't want to intrude on you, Livvy, thanks. Eula and I ate along the way. We just wanted to pick up this scalawag here."

Eula Pendleton put her empty cup on the table and picked up her purse. "Yes, but thank you for the offer." She rose, but Jenny made no move to get up.

"Daddy? The Waltons said I could stay with them for a while."

The statement caught both the Pendletons by surprise. Dave stared at Jenny, then at John and Olivia.

"That's right, Dave," John nodded. "Why don't you let her stay a few days. We were just getten acquainted."

"We'd be real glad to have her," Olivia smiled.

John-Boy's hopes rose cautiously as Dave seemed to consider the idea.

"What this little girls deserves," he said, "is a trip across my knee." He gave Jenny a stern look and then suddenly grinned. "But seein' she's mine and spoiled rotten to boot, Eula and I have decided to open up the old place and stay on for a while."

It was as if a spring had suddenly been released inside everyone in the room. Even Grandma cheered as Jenny leaped to her feet and gave her father another kiss. John-Boy felt like the teetering world had suddenly righted itself again.

"Oh, Dad, thank you," Jenny was crying. "And you too, Eula. You're the nicest parents anybody could have."

"Okay." Dave laughed. "Enough of this nonsense. Let's go take a look at that old barn."

Jenny turned happily to Olivia. "I'll come over first thing in the morning, Mrs. Walton. You just leave the breakfast dishes. And Grandma, I'll hold you to your promise to teach me how to crochet. And I want to help with the polliwogs, Mary Ellen. And—"

"And, and, and." Dave Pendleton laughed. "If you're gonna be up to so much tomorrow, we'd better get started with all that dust in our own house." He put an arm around Jenny. "John, Livvy, I sure appreciate your lookin' after my little girl."

"We enjoyed haven her, Dave."

"And she did far more than her share of work around here."

John-Boy opened the door for them. Jenny gave him a happy, triumphant smile, and John-Boy walked out with her after the others said good-bye.

"Don't forget your promise to take me to the mountain tomorrow, John-Boy."

"I won't forget. In fact, if it's all right, maybe I can come over to your house tonight."

"Could you? I'm sure Dad and Eula would be delighted."

Dave Pendleton was holding the car door open. "Come on, Jenny."

"I have some work to do this afternoon," John-Boy said quickly. "Maybe I can make it after supper."

"Please try," she said and hurried to the car.

"Good-bye, John-Boy," Mr. Pendleton called. "And thanks again."

"Good-bye, Mr. Pendleton."

John-Boy shoved his hands into his pockets and watched as the car made a U-turn and started down the road. In a way he was glad Jenny wasn't going to live with them. Now he wouldn't have to share her with the rest of the family. He quickly pulled out a hand and waved as Jenny smiled at him through the back window.

In the kitchen Olivia and Grandma were putting out bread and pickles and milk. Grandpa was already slicing into a ham, making a sandwich.

"Seems like a real nice girl," he remarked. "A good-looker, too. That Dave Pendleton always did know how to pick 'em." He glanced at Grandma's scowl and quickly added, "Yes sir, that Dave Pendleton's almost as good as I am at pickin' pretty girls."

"Hmmph," Grandma responded and headed for the cupboard to get plates. "I surely do wish I had as good a taste as you did, old man."

It took a minute for the remark to sink in, then everyone laughed and looked at Grandpa. He shook his head.

"I'm not goen to answer that, old lady, you're too quick-tongued for me. Here, John-Boy, have yourself a sandwich."

"Ladies are generally served first," Erin pointed out.

"That's right, and generally I'm the first one to oblige 'em. But John-Boy and me, we got work to do this afternoon. Ain't that right, John-Boy?"

"That's right, Grandpa." John-Boy glanced at his mother and held his breath.

"What do you mean, you're goen to work?"

John-Boy started to speak, not certain what was going to come out of his mouth. But his father quickly winked and came to the rescue. "John-Boy's got a job, Livvy. He's gotta pick up some things at Ike Godsey's and make a delivery. I told John-Boy he could use the truck so long as Grandpa went with him."

The statements were true, but they didn't exactly give an accurate picture of the situation. Grandpa glanced slyly at John-Boy and took a huge bite of sandwich. Olivia looked at both of them, and over at her husband, then turned back to the sink. She appeared a little suspicious, but she didn't pursue the matter.

V

Cousin Homer Lee was seated in a rocking chair with a tall glass in his hand when John-Boy and Grandpa pulled up to the Baldwin house. John-Boy waved to him and carefully backed the truck up to the garage.

"Who's that?" Grandpa asked suspiciously.

"Cousin Homer Lee Baldwin from Buckin'ham County."

"Hmmph! Looks like one o' them tent-show actors."

Cousin Homer Lee had removed his coat, revealing white suspenders with gold clasps, but he still wore his string tie. "Ahhh." He smiled as he brought his drink over to the truck. "Good mornen, John-Boy. The good Lord has blessed us with a fine day, hasn't he."

"Good *afternoon*," Grandpa said pointedly.

"And to you, sir. And whom, may I ask, do I have the pleasure of addressin'?"

"Zebulon Walton of Walton's Mountain, Virginia, sir."

It was clear that Grandpa intended to take no guff

from Cousin Homer Lee. The two men regarded each other with smiling hostility for a minute and then turned their attention to the Baldwin sisters. The two ladies came smiling out of the Recipe room, wiping their hands on aprons.

"Why now, isn't this a treat!" Miss Emily bubbled. "How nice of you, John-Boy, to bring your grandpa!"

"I declare, nobody ever appreciated the Recipe more than Mr. Walton. How nice to see you!"

Grandpa removed a nonexistent hat and bowed. "The pleasure, ladies, is all mine."

"Do come in out of the hot sun, won't you all? We've just been mixin' up some more of Papa's Recipe. Perhaps you'd join us in a sip, Mr. Walton?"

"Indeed, yes, ladies."

"And Cousin Homer Lee, I'm sure you'll be sociable with us and have a drop more?"

"A small drop, perhaps, yes."

Miss Emily rested a hand on Grandpa's arm and they all moved toward the Recipe room. "Cousin Homer Lee's been restin' on the porch this mornen. You see, he's been just exhausted by his travels."

"Miss Mamie?" John-Boy asked. "Where do you want me to put this sugar?"

"Just bring it into the supply room, John-Boy."

The others disappeared inside and John-Boy moved the fifty-pound sacks to the rear of the truck, then carried each of them to the supply room and stacked them in a corner. When the task was completed he went to the Recipe room and waited unobtrusively by the door.

John-Boy had never before been in the room while the ladies were brewing Recipe. The heat and the strong odors surprised him. The big caldron now gurgled and bubbled over an intensely hot charcoal fire. Next to it, endless coils of copper tubing were thick with condensation, and a clear liquid dripped slowly into shallow pans. The sweet-sour aroma made breathing difficult.

"You've done it again," Cousin Homer Lee was saying. He held his glass high, turning it in the light. "An ambrosial nectar of extraordinary quality, ladies."

Grandpa smacked his lips. "Very good, ladies. I'd say the finest you've ever made."

"Oh, it's such a joy to hear menfolks' voices around the place again, isn't it, Mamie. Mr. Walton, you haven't paid us a visit in just ages."

"And isn't it nice that Mr. Walton could meet Cousin Homer Lee," Miss Mamie chimed.

The ladies sipped their Recipe from teacups, their little fingers delicately extended. Grandpa took another drink and eyed Homer Lee.

"I take it you are a businessman, sir?"

"Oh, Cousin Homer Lee is a self-made man," Miss Emily answered. "Left Buckin'ham County with nothen but the clothes on his back, and look at him now!"

"Yes, yes," Cousin Homer Lee added. "Among other things I have dabbled in the field of commerce. Buy low, sell high, that's the secret."

"What is it you buy and sell?" Grandpa asked.

"Goods, commodities, items of commercial value. And what, if I may ask, is your line of endeavor, Mr. Walton?"

Grandpa looked puzzled for a minute, but quickly recovered. "Timber," he said, and seemed pleased with the answer.

"Isn't that wonderful," Miss Emily sighed. "To have two important men of commerce and business in our home at the same time. I declare, Mamie, it's just like when Papa was alive, isn't it!"

Miss Mamie picked up a jar of the Recipe. "Shall we retire to the parlor where we can all be more comfortable?"

John-Boy spent the rest of the afternoon dusting off old pictures and bringing them down from the attic. When all the relatives came for the reunion, Miss Mamie wanted pictures of every family member hanging from the walls. In the parlor voices grew louder and the bursts of laughter more frequent. Cousin Homer Lee, it seemed, was telling about his travels to exotic places like San Francisco and Hollywood and Boston, Massachusetts. Then everybody was clapping hands and singing "Blow the Man Down" while Grandpa did an Irish jig.

It was almost dark when John-Boy got all the pictures down and ready for hanging. The mason jar, he noticed, was now empty and another had been brought in from the Recipe room.

"Grandpa, I think we should be headen on home."

"Home? Why it's only the shank of the evenen, John-Boy."

Cousin Homer pulled a railroad watch from his pocket. "Good Lord, ladies, look at the hour. How time flies in agreeable company. But we'd better hurry along ourselves."

"Oh, dear," Miss Emily gasped, "I plumb forgot all about Cousin Homer taken us to the movies tonight."

Miss Mamie was smiling giddily, pouring more Recipe into her teacup. Another time, Homer Lee. We can go another time. We're havin' such joy here."

"Now, now, you're not goin' to back out this time, Cousin Mamie." Cousin Homer tapped Grandpa on the knee. "Zeb, do you know the last time these ladies saw a picture show?"

"Don't think I do."

Miss Mamie gazed dreamily at the ceiling. "It was when Papa took us to see Mr. Chaplin in *The Gold Rush*. I can remember it like it was just yesterday."

"Grandpa?" John-Boy said, but no one heard him.

"Papa just loved the part where Charlie ate the shoe!" Miss Emily exclaimed.

"There you are," Cousin Homer said. "Why, that was from the silent days. I'll wager you've never seen one of the new talken pictures."

"We thought the silents were just fine, Cousin Homer."

"But you mustn't judge until you've heard the talkies. And we'd better get started so we don't come in at the middle."

Grandpa struggled to his feet. "John-Boy, we'd better be getten along too. Ladies, it's been a grand evenen."

The sisters went for their coats. "Do come again, Mr.

Walton. Some time when Cousin Homer isn't rushin' us off somewhere."

"Thank you, I will do that."

"John-Boy," Miss Emily smiled, "would you be so kind as to offer me your arm?"

Cousin Homer led the way to the garage while Grandpa and John-Boy escorted the ladies on their arms.

"I do wish you and John-Boy were comin' along," Miss Mamie said. "Wouldn't that be jolly, sister?"

"Yes. And we must all remember to keep an eye open for Ashley Longworth." Miss Emily squeezed John-Boy's arm and smiled. "Ashley was the young gentleman who came courtin' some years ago."

"I'm sure he was a real nice man, Miss Emily."

"Just as handsome as you can imagine, John-Boy."

"Well, toodle-oo, you-all," Miss Mamie waved, and settled herself in the car.

Miss Emily slipped two dollars into John-Boy's hand and took her place in the back seat beside her sister. They both waved, and Grandpa and John-Boy backed away to watch the departure.

"Fine ladies," Grandpa said a little mushily. "Fine ladies."

A low growl came from the car's self-starter. There was silence and then the growl came again. This time it continued, growing weaker and weaker until it was almost inaudible.

John-Boy's heart sank. They were already late for supper. If the Baldwin sisters' car didn't start it would mean another half hour of fooling around to make it run. That might make it impossible for him to go to Jenny's house tonight.

The starter gave two more feeble grunts and then was silent.

"It's no use, Homer," Grandpa called. "Sounds to me like the battery's dead."

Miss Emily's head came out a window. "Are you sure we've got gasoline?"

Miss Mamie's head came out the other window. "We can use the Recipe if there's no gas. Papa used to use it all the time."

"Trouble's with the battery, Miss Mamie," Grandpa said. "I'm afraid she's not goin' anywheres tonight."

John-Boy followed Grandpa into the garage, feeling a dark premonition about what was going to happen. From the moment they had carried that mason jar into the parlor, he knew the day was going to have a bad ending.

"Oh dear," Miss Emily said as they all got out of the car, "I just wish the idea had never come up. I had my heart set on seein' a moven-picture show."

"I did too," Miss Mamie echoed. "I just can hardly believe that actors talk and sing right out loud."

John-Boy winced as Grandpa smiled and gestured gallantly toward the truck. "There's nothen to worry about, ladies. You're goen to Charlottesville after all."

"Oh, Mr. Walton, we couldn't!"

Miss Emily studied the truck for a second and smiled happily. "Yes, we can, Mamie. There's plenty of room if Cousin Homer and Mr. Walton ride in the back."

"Grandpa," John-Boy protested, "they're expectin' us at home!"

It was no use. Grandpa was already escorting the ladies to the truck. "And home we'll be," he said. "Just a little late, John-Boy."

"Isn't this a treat?" Miss Emily said.

"Yes, you can always depend on the Walton men!"

Grandpa climbed into the back of the truck and John-Boy trudged resignedly toward the cab. It seemed that every time he was around the Baldwin sisters he was trapped into doing something he didn't want to do. He wondered if he would ever have the courage to refuse them.

"Haven't changed your mind, have you, Cousin Homer?" Grandpa called out.

Cousin Homer was still standing in the garage as if uncertain about the change in plans. He suddenly reached into the back seat of the Baldwins' car and brought out an old suitcase. "Certainly not," he said and carried the bag to the truck. "You don't mind if I drop this off in town, do you? It's just some dirty laundry."

There was a definite clinking sound as he swung the heavy bag up to the truck bed. Laundry? John-Boy stared for a minute, but Cousin Homer smiled and waved them on.

"Let's go, John-Boy, we don't want to be late."

The movie was Billy-Jack Bibb in *Rhythm of the Rockies,* and John-Boy might have enjoyed it under different circumstances. His first preoccupation was his mother's concern and the worry she would be experiencing when he and grandpa didn't come home. Then his thoughts turned to Jenny Pendleton and grim speculations about what she would think when he didn't show up at her house. For John-Boy the movie seemed endless, and each time Billy-Jack Bibb picked up his guitar and began singing he slouched deeper and more miserably into his seat.

Next to him, Grandpa and the Baldwin sisters enjoyed it thoroughly. The ladies oohed and aahed at the Rocky Mountain scenery, and gleefully sang along with Billy-Jack and his guitar, while Grandpa grunted his approval or shouted warnings to Billy-Jack when the villain was approaching.

Cousin Homer Lee Baldwin didn't go to the movie. When they arrived at the theater he groaned and shook his head, saying he'd already seen the picture three times. But he insisted they all go on in, and he'd find something to do in town and be back when the picture was over. He also insisted on paying the admission for all four of them, and then he walked off carrying his suitcase.

John-Boy wondered if it was all worth it. He had earned three dollars so far. But it would be impossible to earn twenty dollars from the Baldwin sisters without his mother finding out where he went every day. And how many more times would he end up in movie theaters, or maybe off in Richmond if Cousin Homer Lee and the ladies drank more of that Recipe?

The picture finally came to an end. Grandpa and the Baldwin sisters stood up and clapped as if expecting the actors to walk out on the stage and take bows.

Then the lights came on and they filed slowly up the aisle with the other patrons.

"I declare, I never saw the likes of it in all my life," Miss Emily exclaimed. "And when he sang 'Springtime in the Rockies' I felt like that young man was singin' the song just for me!"

"We must come back again, Emily. I don't remember havin' such a nice evenin'. Did you enjoy it, John-Boy?"

"It was very good, Miss Mamie."

Cousin Homer was waiting in the lobby, and once they were in the truck and headed home, John-Boy heard every verse of "Springtime in the Rockies" four more times.

They dropped off Cousin Homer and the Baldwin sisters, and it was almost midnight when John-Boy finally stopped the truck in front of the barn and roused Grandpa. Every light in the house was ablaze, and Sheriff Bridges's old Ford was parked in front of the house.

"They'll never even see us, John-Boy," Grandpa said. "We'll just tiptoe through the back door and up the stairs."

"I think it's too late, Grandpa."

"It's never too late, son. Just follow me."

John-Boy knew better. Reckless was barking happily, and the screen door at the back was already open, John-Boy's father peering out.

" 'Lo there, John," Grandpa said. "Beautiful night, isn't it."

"Yes it is, Grandpa."

Grandpa went through the door, and John-Boy glimpsed his father's rueful smile as he followed him in.

"Kind of late, son."

"I know, Daddy."

The faces of those sitting at the kitchen table didn't appear so amiable. His mother looked relieved, but her jaw quickly tightened. Sitting across from her, Sheriff Bridges was idly stirring coffee, watching through narrowed eyes, and Grandma was already on her feet, pointing toward the stairs.

"I'll have a word with you, old man!"

Grandpa smiled at the Sheriff and surveyed the group as if pleased by the reception. "In due time, old woman. First, I'll have a cup of coffee if there's any made, Livvy."

"It's on the stove."

"Fine. I'll just serve myself, Livvy. No need for you to get up. You're all up a little late for Sunday night, aren't you?"

Grandpa's airy manner was having no effect on the others. John-Boy slipped into a chair and glanced at Ep Bridges, wondering how long ago he had been called and where he might have searched for them. The Sheriff was smiling quietly at him.

"How you keepin', John-Boy?"

"Fine and dandy, Sheriff."

"Glad to hear that. You been over to Charlottesville lately?"

All eyes were on him now, with only Grandpa smiling, scooping sugar into his coffee. John-Boy nodded. "We was over there tonight. We . . . uh, saw a picture show."

He saw his mother's mouth open and close again.

"I was with the boy, Sheriff," Grandpa said. "He's been up to no mischief."

"Y'all had yourselves a good time, huh?"

Grandpa grinned. "As a matter of fact we did. We—"

"With no thought of folks at home," Grandma interrupted. "Ever'body worried sick about where you might be!"

"Don't tell me you've had the Sheriff out looken for us?"

John Walton's quiet voice came from the end of the table. "We should have. But the Sheriff's here on business of his own. John-Boy, your mother and I have been out looken for you all night. Up to the Baldwin house and half-dozen other places. I hope you got a good story to tell us."

John-Boy glanced at his mother, understanding now the cold fury of her expression. His father must have told her about his job with the Baldwin sisters. But at the moment the Sheriff concerned him more. Did his business have something to do with Jenny?

"Now just a minute," Grandpa said. "Before anybody goes jumpen on the boy, I want it understood it was all my fault."

"I coulda guessed that easy enough," Grandma nodded. "We're listenen, old man."

"Well, you see it was this way. The Baldwin sisters had their hearts set on goen to town and their car wasn't worken. So we took 'em in the truck. That's all there is to it."

Grandma shook her head. "One of 'em too young to be sowin' wild oats and the other too old, but that don't stop 'em. I just don't know about these Walton men."

"Son," John Walton said, "if there's been any wild-oat sowin', maybe I'd better hear about it."

"We just went to a picture show, Daddy."

"Billy-Jack Bibb, the Croonin' Cowhand." Grandpa grinned.

John nodded. "Sheriff, you got some questions you want to ask these two?"

Sheriff Bridges was listening thoughtfully. Now he gave each of them a sharp glance. "I got word from the law in Charlottesville that somebody's suspected of transportin' bootleg whiskey in your truck. You know anythin' about that?"

John-Boy's heart jumped, but he said nothing, staring blankly at the Sheriff. A charge like that was ridiculous. They had taken the truck to the movies and come directly home.

His mother shook her head. "I'm surprised you're both not in jail."

"Is John-Boy goin' to jail?"

The alarmed question came from the living room, and for the first time John-Boy saw the row of faces peering through the stairway posts. Elizabeth was on the verge of tears. "I don't want John-Boy to go to jail," she whimpered.

Livvy was instantly on her feet. "Back to bed! All of you, this instant!" She shooed them all up the stairs, then came back when she was certain they were gone.

"John-Boy," his father said, "do you know anythin' about any whiskey bein' sold from my truck tonight?"

"No, Daddy, we were all at the picture show. All but Cousin Homer Lee. He—"

The recollection of the suitcase and the way it had clinked when Cousin Homer swung it up to the truck bed suddenly hit John-Boy. He swallowed hard and went on. "He . . . he didn't go to the show."

Sheriff Bridges's eyes narrowed. "Would that be Cousin Homer Lee Baldwin from Buckin'ham County, John-Boy?"

"Yes, he's visiten the Baldwin sisters."

A half smile came to the sheriff's face. "Oh-oh," he said.

"What's that mean?" John asked.

"That means things are startin' to make a little sense around here." Sheriff Bridges smiled. "Cousin Homer Lee Baldwin's got a record that would stretch from here to Rockfish."

"Good heavens!" Grandma cried. Grandpa was blinking at the Sheriff in total disbelief.

"Maybe we ought to say somethin' to Miss Emily and Miss Mamie," John-Boy said.

The Sheriff shook his head. "What I'd rather you do, son, is keep an eye on Fourth Cousin Homer Lee. We don't have any solid evidence yet. The whiskey showed up at Daisy Burgess's beauty parlor over in Charlottesville, but I don't think we can pin it on Cousin Homer Lee unless we can catch him with some in his possession. Or sellin' it."

Olivia's jaw had tightened again. "Sheriff, I'd just rather John-Boy wouldn't be spendin' so much time at the Baldwins'."

"I see your point, Livvy. But I'd appreciate it if you'd change your mind. I know you wouldn't like to see that Recipe of the Baldwins bein' sold all over the county."

Olivia gazed despairingly at the Sheriff for a minute, then turned to John. The dilemma was beyond her.

"The boy knows how to take care of himself, Livvy," John said.

"Hangin' around over there. Next thing you know he'll be drinken whiskey!"

"I won't drink any whiskey, Mama," John-Boy protested.

"You just keep an eye open, John-Boy," Sheriff Bridges said. "First sign of any funny business, you call me on the telephone."

"We haven't got a telephone, Sheriff. I never used one."

The Sheriff got his hat. "Ike's got one down at the store. If you have any trouble, he'll show you how to use it."

Grandma was on her feet the minute the door closed behind the Sheriff. Grandpa got up slowly and followed after her. "You ought to see that picture, old woman," he said as they headed up the stairs. "That Billy-Jack Bibb can really sing a song." Grandma's answer was lost behind the bang of a door.

In the silence John-Boy looked over at his mother. She looked weary, but her expression had softened.

"I'm sorry, Mama. I tried to come home. And I promise I won't go near any of that whiskey."

For a minute he thought she was going to cry. But then she smiled gently and put her hand on his father's. "I know you won't, John-Boy."

"Better go on up to bed, son," his father said.

"Good night, Daddy. Good night, Mama."

John-Boy headed for his room but stopped at the bottom of the stairs. "Did anythin' happen around here this afternoon?" he asked, "Or around suppertime?"

"No," his father said. "You expectin' somethin' to happen?"

"No," John-Boy said. "Good night."

It was silly to expect Jenny to come over to his house, he thought as he put on his pajamas. He really hadn't promised that he would visit her after supper. He'd said he would try. But she would have been expecting him. And when he didn't show up it would certainly indicate that he hadn't tried very hard.

John-Boy slid under the covers and sighed deeply. And what would he tell her tomorrow? That he couldn't come because he went to a picture show with the Baldwin sisters? On the other hand, he reflected, there was now an element of romance attached to his working for the Baldwin sisters. He was on a special assignment for Sheriff Ep Bridges. He smiled at the idea, but then quickly dismissed it. Keeping an eye on Cousin Homer Lee Baldwin didn't exactly make him a high-level secret agent. And telling Jenny Pendleton such a thing was likely to prompt laughter rather than admiration.

The only thing, he finally decided, was to tell her the truth.

VI

There were none of the usual subdued sounds of early morning when John-Boy woke up. And instead of the predawn darkness, the sun streamed brilliantly through his window. John-Boy sat up with alarm, his first thought being that he would be late for school. Then he smiled and dropped back to the pillow. It was Monday, but it was spring vacation.

From outside the window he could hear the squeals and laughter of the other children, and then the long screech of his father's saw cutting down the length of a board. Apparently everyone else had been up for hours. Jenny! he suddenly thought. She was probably downstairs waiting for him. He jumped from the bed and hurriedly dressed.

"Good morning, John-Boy," Jenny said happily when he came in the kitchen. The table was cleared and the dishes done, and Jenny was helping his mother shell peas. She looked more beautiful than ever in a fresh white blouse and flowered skirt. "Your mother wanted to wake you up, but I wouldn't let her. She's been telling me all about how she and your father met each other. Did you know they were childhood sweethearts? I think that's wonderful."

Olivia smiled and got out a skillet and John-Boy sat down, not knowing exactly how to respond to Jenny's bubbling manner. He wondered if she were angry with him and was trying to cover it up. "You should have woke me up."

"Well, after last night I guess you could use some extra sleep," his mother chuckled. She dropped three slices of bacon into the skillet and got out the pitcher of milk.

"You didn't forget about taking me up to Walton's Mountain, did you?" Jenny asked.

"No, I didn't forget." He smiled at her, but Jenny quickly turned her attention back to the peas.

"Are the other children goen with you-all?" his mother asked.

John-Boy caught the anxious undertone in her voice. But the last thing he wanted was a crowd of little kids around. He had lots of explaining to do to Jenny, and once that was over he was looking forward to being alone with her. "Well—"

"We'll be glad to take them along, Mrs. Walton. I think it would be fun. Don't you, John-Boy?"

While he ate breakfast his mother and Jenny talked about how the Pendletons were planning to redecorate their house. Jenny bubbled excitedly over curtain colors and new carpeting, and how she was going to plant a garden just like the Waltons had out in back. John-Boy ate silently, and neither his mother nor Jenny seemed to notice. When he finished Jenny jumped up and took his plate to the sink, but his mother waved her away.

"Don't bother with those, I'll do them. You just get the other children and run along."

"Thank you, Mrs. Walton. And we won't stay too long." She gave John-Boy a fleeting smile and headed for the door.

John-Boy was certain she was angry now. She had avoided looking at him a half dozen times, and her gay manner was far too exaggerated. When he went out the back door she was already talking to the other children.

Mary Ellen, Ben, Jim-Bob, and Elizabeth had dug a huge hole in the backyard, and were now leveling the bottom, scooping out the last of the loose dirt.

"It's a frog pond," Mary Ellen was telling Jenny. "When they get a little bigger, we'll have to dig more holes, of course. We'll probably need twenty or thirty holes like this before the frogs are big enough to sell."

"If they don't all die first," Erin said. She had her arms folded, peering cynically into the hole.

"They're not goen to die," Elizabeth said defiantly.

"Don't pay any attention to her," Mary Ellen said. "Jim-Bob, get the hose. We're goen to fill her up."

"How many tadpoles do you have?" Jenny asked.

"Three hundred for this hole. Come on everybody, out!"

Jenny seemed to be absorbed by the operation, and John-Boy watched as Jim-Bob turned on the hose and dragged it over. When the water began gurgling into the pit John-Boy glanced around.

"You-all are so busy I guess none of you wants to go up on the mountain, do you?"

"Can't," Ben said matter-of-factly. "Got too much work."

"We're not going to be long," Jenny said. "And we'd love to have you."

No one seemed to hear her. Jim-Bob looked anxiously at Mary Ellen. "Can we put the tadpoles in yet?"

"Not yet. Water's still too muddy."

Ben lifted his dirty hands and turned them over. "Yuuch, I'm all muddy too."

Jim-Bob moved without warning. The hose whipped out of the pit and, grinning, he swung it toward Ben. "This'll clean you off!"

Erin stumbled, backing away, and Jenny quickly stepped to the side avoiding the spray from Jim-Bob's wild swinging of the hose. Everyone was suddenly shouting, with Mary Ellen screaming loudest for Jim-Bob to look out for the tadpoles. But the warning came too late. The hose dragged across the jar, and what looked like a million tadpoles suddenly gushed across the dirt and began squirming around in the mud.

"Jim-Bob, you dumb . . . ! Get 'em! Pick 'em up! Fast!"

Then everyone was on his knees in the mud, shouting, scooping tadpoles toward the water in the hole. John-Boy quietly touched Jenny's elbow. "Let's go."

"But shouldn't we help?"

"No," John-Boy said. "It's too crowded already."

Jenny glanced from John-Boy to the mud, then moved hesitantly away. Mary Ellen's voice followed them as they finally headed down the road. "How am I goen to get rich with you bunch of idiots around? Get the hose back in there, Jim-Bob! Elizabeth! There's one right by your foot! Don't step on it!"

From the kitchen window Olivia groaned inwardly as she watched the frenzy of bodies jumping in and out of the mud. In two minutes the six kids were dirtying enough overalls and dresses and socks to keep her scrubbing for the rest of the day. Even Erin and Jason, who professed to have no interest in getting rich with frogs' legs, were now splattered from head to toe.

But as distressing as was the scene at the muddy frog pond, Olivia gazed even more anxiously at the road where John-Boy and Jenny Pendleton were walking away.

It was obvious what had happened. The other children were too occupied with the frogs to have any interest in going up to Walton's Mountain. She should have expected as much. But the idea of two maturing teen-agers going off by themselves—

She bit indecisively at her lip and leaned closer to the window in an effort to see if John was out by the barn. But this was silly, she decided. She rinsed the last of the dishes, placed them on the drainboard, and got the dish towel.

When a boy reached a certain age, it was ridiculous for a mother to worry about whether he behaved himself or not. His character was well formed long before the age of seventeen, and he either knew right from wrong, or he didn't. And there was nothing anybody could do about it. Would she continue to worry and watch out for John-Boy when he was eighteen, or nineteen, or twenty-one? Of course not. At some point she must face the issue courageously, and she must let the chips fall where they may.

And Jenny Pendleton— Olivia chewed lightly at her lip again as she thought about the girl. Jenny was very pretty, and as sweet and wholesome as she could be. But it was also obvious that she was quite taken by John-Boy. When he came down for breakfast she had babbled on and on, as nervous as a cat. But she was a sensible girl. She certainly wouldn't let things get out of hand with John-Boy.

But what if something should happen? Those things happened so easily. Children might have no intention of doing anything wrong. They might be the finest children in the world, and have the finest of feelings and the best Christian upbringing. But nature was a powerful thing. And subtle. Oh, Lord, it was subtle and devious at times.

Olivia dried her hands, hung the dish towel neatly on its rack, and took a deep breath. It was probably useless to talk to John about these things. She had a good idea what he would say. Still, she had to have a clear conscience in the matter. She fixed a smile on her face and marched as casually as she could out the back door and across the yard.

"John," she said when he finished cutting a heavy piece of lumber, "John-Boy has gone up to the mountain with Jenny Pendleton."

He had turned off the saw motor and was smiling triumphantly as he ran his hand over the surface of the wood. "That so? Look at this piece of oak, Livvy girl. You don't get many oak timbers this size. Likely bring two dollars down in Charlottesville."

Olivia watched him as he bent forward and sighted along the smooth edge of the timber. It was obvious he had no idea what she was talking about.

"John-Boy and Jenny went up to the mountain alone. I tried to get them to take some of the other children, but they're too busy with their tadpoles."

John glanced over at the children. "Yep. Looks like we're goen to have a backyard full of mudholes all summer."

"John?"

"What's the matter, Livvy?"

His sudden grin revealed that he knew exactly what she was talking about. Olivia stood perfectly still as he put an arm around her, kissed her lightly on the back of the neck, and moved to the far end of the timber.

"Yep," he said, "I guess I could follow 'em up the mountain and make sure nothen happens. That wouldn't be too much trouble. Then I can follow 'em around all day tomorrow. And I can follow John-Boy out there to the Baldwins' and make sure he don't touch any of that whiskey." He grinned. "Or, better yet, we could lock John-Boy up till he's twenty-one. Come to think of it, maybe that's what my daddy should have done when I first met you, Livvy."

Olivia couldn't help smiling. John was right; at some time or another a few risks had to be taken. But she still ached for reassurance. "Do you really think it'll be all right?"

"I don't know. That Jenny Pendleton is a city girl, and from what I hear they're pretty fast. I sure hope she don't take advantage of one of us country folk."

"John, I do wish you'd be serious sometimes."

He came toward her, grinning. "Sometimes I'm so serious, Livvy, I can't stand it." He squeezed her hard and kissed her on the mouth. Olivia didn't resist and he kissed her four or five times before he let her go.

As she straightened her dress and headed back to the house, Olivia felt some measure of reassurance. In his crazy way, John always seemed more sensible about things like this. Then, as she opened the screen door, she glanced over at the mudhole and felt herself flush deeply. The children were all staring at her, every one of them wearing a silly grin on his face.

To John-Boy, the chance of anything terrible happening with Jenny seemed extremely remote as they walked along the road. She kept well away from him, and her eyes flitted from trees and wild flowers to clouds and distant houses—everywhere but to him. All this was accompanied by a steady stream of chatter that John-Boy responded to with nods and murmurs of assent.

"You're very quiet today, John-Boy," she finally said as they started up the side of the mountain.

"I'm not getten much chance to say anythen."

She smiled coolly to that. "Yes, I guess I do talk too much, don't I."

"I wanted to explain why I didn't come over last night. And tell you I'm sorry."

"You don't have to explain," she shrugged. "In fact I really didn't expect you at all."

"But I—"

She suddenly scampered up a steep slope and broke into a run. "I'll bet I can beat you to the top," she called, and was gone, loping off into the forest.

John-Boy stood perfectly still for a minute, watching her. The first spring needles were coming out at the tips of the pine branches, and the new green oak leaves were brilliantly transparent in the dappled sunlight. John-Boy watched Jenny duck under branches and then disappear among the thickening trees. He knew she could not keep up that pace for long, and he moved slowly and steadily up the slope.

Five minutes later he was startled by a voice from the side and behind him.

"What's your hurry?"

It was Jenny. She was sitting on a shaded rock, her chin cupped in her hands and breathing heavily.

"It's only a half mile more," he smiled.

"Why didn't you tell me it was so far. Go on ahead if you want."

"No, I'd rather go with you."

She smiled, but quickly controlled it, looking off at the top of the mountain. "All right, let's go."

After they had walked another hundred yards John-Boy glanced over at her. "The reason I couldn't come last night was because I was worken."

She made no response, her eyes fixed on the path ahead.

"I wanted to come, and I tried as hard as I could to

get away. I've been worken for the Baldwin sisters. I've been tryen to earn enough money to buy Mama a washen machine."

Jenny shrugged lightly, as if such information was of no interest to her.

"Anyhow, I didn't get home till almost midnight. I expect that's why I slept so late this mornen. I felt awful about not maken it over to see you."

Jenny was silent for another minute, then looked far ahead. "Is that the top of the mountain?"

"Yes it is."

She smiled as if to herself and suddenly broke into long strides again. John-Boy kept within ten yards of her this time, all the while wondering what might be going on in her head. If Jenny Pendleton were his sister, Mary Ellen, or Erin, there would never be any doubts over what she was thinking about. Those two never hesitated to let people know their opinions. But Jenny was a complete mystery to him. One minute she talked a blue streak and the next minute she was a sphinx. John-Boy wondered if there was something else he had done that might be disturbing her.

The only things left from the original Walton cabin were parts of the foundation, the old stone fireplace and chimney, and a few rotted logs. As she approached, Jenny slowed her pace, and then moved reverently into the weed-grown site.

"Is this it?" she breathed.

"Uh-huh." John-Boy moved to her side and stuck his hands in his pockets. He had been here so many times he no longer had any strong reactions to the place. His father had often talked about rebuilding it and moving the family back up the mountain. But the hard times of the Depression had postponed the idea so long it no longer seemed real.

"What a marvelous old chimney," Jenny said quietly. She stepped carefully over a log and stood in what would have been the center of the cabin. "Just think, a man and a woman once stood right there and warmed themselves in front of the fire. And children played here on the floor." She shook her head. "Why I'll bet the woman cooked right there in the fireplace!"

"Probably," John-Boy said. "Everythin' was make-do back in those days."

Jenny moved to a far corner, then turned around, surveying the area. "What were their names?"

"His was Rome. Hers was Rebecca-Lee."

Jenny smiled and crossed to the hearth of the fireplace. She reached in, as if stirring something in a huge cooking pot, then looked sternly over at him.

"Rome Walton, your supper's ready!"

John-Boy stared at her for a minute, then stepped over a log and crouched, as if defending the cabin with a rifle. "Can't come right now, Becky-Lee! Indians attackin'!"

"My sakes! Are there many of 'em?"

John-Boy swung the rifle, tracking an imaginary target. "Pow, pow! Pow! Not any more, Becky-Lee. I think that's the lot."

"You better come to supper now. I can't keep this venison warm much longer."

John-Boy gave her a sour look. "Venison! Again tonight?"

"I just cook what you bring to the house, Rome. You want bear steak for a change, you'd better go out and shoot yourself a bear!"

"I shot a bear yesterday! Don't you remember that one chased you across the cornfield?"

"Bless my soul! I plumb forgot about that one. So many bears been chasin' me lately I just can't keep track anymore. Well, I'll throw this venison to the wolves out there and cook you up some bear."

John-Boy marched across the cabin with the exaggerated gait of a burly frontier hunter. "Becky-Lee, you're a good old pioneer lady."

Jenny's stern manner suddenly softened as she looked up him. Her voice was barely a whisper. "And you're a good old pioneer man, Rome Walton."

John-Boy was hardly conscious of taking her in his arms. The game was over, but in playing it they had said wonderful things to each other. Becky-Lee and Rome Walton had endured the hardships of settling virgin land in a hostile environment and in their experiences Jenny Pendleton and John-Boy Walton had found a tender, enduring bond. Their long kiss, and then holding each other seemed as natural and uncomplicated as might have been the embrace of the cabin's original occupants.

"I felt terrible last night, John-Boy," Jenny murmured, "I thought something might have happened to you. Or that you didn't care. Or that I might never see you again."

John-Boy held her closer, not trusting his voice. He gently stroked her hair, and then smiled at her as she looked up. He kissed her again, then kissed her cheeks and nose and forehead. "It'll never happen again, Jenny. Never again. Nobody's ever goen to keep us apart again."

For another minute they held the embrace. Then Jenny drew gently away and looked at the fireplace. She pushed a lock of hair from her forehead and laughed nervously. "Well, I guess I'd better get these dishes done."

"To heck with the dishes," John-Boy said. He took her hand and headed toward the nonexistent front door. "You been worken hard for 'leven years now, Becky-Lee Walton. It's time you enjoyed the scenery around here."

"But how about the wolves and bears? And Indians?"

"No need to worry about them. I got my rifle and powder."

John-Boy had no idea what happened to the next two hours. Nor was he certain about whether Jenny Pendleton was really Jenny Pendleton or Becky-Lee Walton, and whether he was John-Boy or Rome Walton. It didn't make a whole lot of difference. The girl who held his hand laughed and smiled and sometimes stopped for no apparent reason and kissed him. As abruptly, she ran away, and reappeared giggling in some hidden glen. They lay on their stomachs and drank water from fresh springs, and they took off their shoes and waded through cool, shaded ponds. Birds chirped and sometimes screeched angrily at them, and a deer watched suspiciously as they sat on a huge rock overlooking the valley.

John-Boy saw places on Walton's Mountain he'd never known existed, and each of them seemed beautiful and lush with the sparkling warmth of spring. And more beautiful than all of them was Jenny's smile, the soft texture of her hair, and the liquid, dancing warmth of her dark-brown eyes. John-Boy held her close to him, and felt his heart clamoring with urgent desire. And there was a moment in which each of them stopped breathing, as if poised on the rim of a deep chasm. But they had closed their eyes and the danger passed.

They must have walked at least five miles. Or maybe it was ten. They had gone down the back of the mountain, through moist-green meadows and virgin forests, and then circled slowly toward home, feeling no obligations to time or place or other people. When, finally, they reached the dirt road and the house came into view, John-Boy released Jenny's hand.

"I guess it must be about lunchtime," he said.

She smiled, understanding the need for caution. She touched her hair, feeling the wild flower John-Boy had placed there, and quickly removed it. But then she changed her mind. She put the flower back, hooked her arm through John-Boy's with a final, quick smile, and then they continued with a respectable distance between them.

It seemed incredible that everything at the Walton house was very much the same as they had left it. The frog pond was now filled, but the same mud-splattered people still surrounded it. Most of them were kneeling, watching the erratic activities of their captives.

"Where you been, John-Boy?" Jason asked.

"Oh, we just walked up to the top of the mountain."

Mary Ellen gave Jenny a hard look. "You goen to help with the tadpoles?"

"I'd like to. What can I do?"

"Nothen now. But we'll be collectin' some more after lunch. And we'll have to dig another hole." Mary Ellen was making it clear that Jenny would get no part of the six million dollars unless she started pulling her weight.

"Children!" Olivia called from the back door. "Lunch is ready. And please don't track that mud into the house." She started to close the door, but then held it open for Jenny and John-Boy. "Did you have a nice time?"

It was silly, John-Boy guessed, but it seemed like his mother was looking at him extra hard.

"Oh, it was beautiful up there," Jenny said. "And so exciting to see where the first Waltons settled."

"You certainly were up there a long time."

Jenny laughed. "John-Boy was pretending to be Rome Walton, fighting off wolves and wild Indians. He killed hundreds of them."

Olivia smiled, her fears suddenly gone. "Well, you two better wash up. You are going to have lunch with us, aren't you, Jenny?"

"Oh, I'd love to."

"Mama," John-Boy asked, "do you think it would be all right if Jenny went with me to the Baldwins' this afternoon?"

"I'm not in favor of anybody goen to the Baldwins', John-Boy."

"But you remember what Sheriff Bridges said last night. He's kind of dependen on me."

Olivia glanced at the two hopeful faces and got butter from the refrigerator. She had heard of no instances in which the Baldwin sisters had corrupted women or girls. Maybe it would be safer for John-Boy to have Jenny along. "I guess it'd be all right. But if you're goen there to work, I don't imagine the Baldwin ladies will appreciate your spendin' the time talken to Jenny."

"Oh, I won't bother him, Mrs. Walton. And maybe I can help find out something about Cousin Homer Lee."

"That kind of business is best left to Sheriff Bridges. I just hope he gets it over with fast."

VII

"Why, of co'se! You're Dave Pendleton's little girl, aren't you! Mamie, look who John-Boy Walton's brought with him this mornen! Young Jennifer Pendleton! My, isn't this a treat and a surprise. You two just come on into the parlor and sit right down. And Jenny Pendleton, aren't you just the prettiest thing! I declare you're as pretty as your dear mother, bless her sainted soul. And John-Boy, I just do believe you're courten this pretty little thing, aren't you. You just sit right over there in the love seat while I see if we don't have some lemonade in the icebox."

Miss Mamie carried on the welcome while Miss Emily went for the lemonade. She had Jenny stand in the middle of the room so she could have a good look at her, and then asked about her father and her new stepmother. "And isn't it nice that you two young people found each other. I declare I sometimes believe such things are all written right down for us in the stars." She sighed happily and Miss Emily arrived with the lemonade.

"Isn't this the most frightful mess!" Miss Emily said when they were all settled. On the low table between them were stacks of lavender-colored envelopes and stationery, along with a bottle of ink and a quill pen. "Sister and I have been writing invitations for the family reunion, and there are just so many of them I declare I'm just ovahwhelmed. Just ovahwhelmed!"

Miss Mamie smiled reprovingly. "There wouldn't be so many, Emily, if we limited our guests solely to family members."

"I still say Ashley Longworth is practically a family member, Mamie. A young man on the very verge, just the very *verge* of proposen, is far more than a friend."

"But you don't even know where he is."

"He attended the University of Virginia. Surely they must have kept track of him."

Jenny sipped her lemonade, delighted with the conversation. "I'm sure the university would forward the letter."

"There you are," Miss Emily said triumphantly, and picked up the pen.

"Well, if you really feel you want to see him after all these years, you just go right ahead." Miss Mamie sighed.

"It is not my desire to see him that is so important, as hurten poor Ashley's feelin's if he should hear we had a grand party and he did not receive an invitation." Miss Emily smiled dreamily. "He had such lovely cheekbones! Don't you remember Ashley Longworth's cheekbones, Mamie?"

"No, I don't remember Ashley's cheekbones, sister." Miss Mamie smiled. "But I do remember he had nice eyes. One was green and one was blue."

"Yes. Think of it. If I had married Ashley this place would be overrun with a whole passel of little children with blue-green eyes." She frowned over at John-Boy. "Some day, young man, would you bring all those brothers and sisters of yours over for a visit? I just adore children."

John-Boy had finished the lemonade and placed the

glass on the corner of the table. "Yes'm. I sure will."

"And be sure to have your Granddaddy Zebulon come along. He does so appreciate our Recipe."

John-Boy nodded. "Miss Mamie, are there any jobs you'll be wanten me to do today?"

"Oh my, yes. The fire could do with more wood, and we'll be needen more jars for the Recipe, and—oh dear, I forgot all about Cousin Homer Lee. Now isn't that rude of me. Cousin Homer's just been worken himself to the bone in the Recipe room, and we haven't even introduced him to Jenny." Her voice rose an octave and she sang out: "Cousin Homer Lee!"

Cousin Homer looked annoyed when he appeared. But the scowl quickly turned to a broad smile when he saw there was company.

"Cousin Homer Lee, you must come in here and meet Miss Jennifer Pendleton. Cousin Homer Lee is from Buckin'ham County, dear."

"Jennifer," Cousin Homer said. "A most charmin' name for an even more charmin' young lady."

"Why, thank you, Mr. Baldwin."

John-Boy smiled as Cousin Homer bowed and kissed Jenny's hand. The sour aroma of the Recipe room had followed him in, and there was a dark stain down the side of his white pants.

"Isn't he just the world's biggest flatterer," Miss Emily gushed. "He just keeps Mamie and me all atwitter around here."

"Any flattery is but a pale mirror of your true beauty, ladies. If I were a poet I should have to venture no farther than Walton's Mountain and this enchanted cottage for a lifetime of inspiration."

Emily sighed. "And he just goes on and on and on. But I declare I could listen to it forever."

Cousin Homer gave her an indulgent smile, then turned serious. "I'm afraid we have a small problem in the Recipe room, ladies. I seem to have added a double portion of sugar to this batch."

"Again!"

Miss Mamie shook her head, amused. "Now isn't that just like Cousin Homer. That's the third time he's made the same mistake. I'm afraid he's just not suited to this kind of work."

"Well," Miss Emily said, "we'll just have to increase all the other ingredients and make a double batch again."

"Yes," Cousin Homer agreed. "And we'll need more jars, of course."

Miss Emily smiled at Jenny. "We've just bought every jar Mr. Godsey has, and they're all gone already. Isn't that just the limit?"

"May I see the Recipe room?" Jenny asked.

"Why, of course you can, Jenny. We'd better get those ingredients all straightened out anyway."

John-Boy had no desire to go into the Recipe room again, but he followed them all through the kitchen and out the side door.

The room was hotter and the odors even more pungent than on John-Boy's first visit. The gurgling caldron was almost overflowing now, and a half-dozen milk cans full of Recipe stood in the far corner.

Miss Mamie explained how the ingredients were mixed and the "base nectar" was distilled from the mash. When she finished she looked at the milk cans and shook her head. "Dear me, I think we're goen to need far more than six dozen mason jars. I think at least twelve dozen, don't you, Mamie?"

"That's how many've been ordered," John-Boy said.

"Oh? I thought it was six. Well, that's just fine. Mr. Godsey should certainly have them by tomorrow."

"And up there on those shelves," Miss Emily went on, "is where we put the jars when they're full. Of course we wash them out and use them over and over again. One can't afford to be wasteful these days. And the Recipe sterilizes them just as pure as they can be."

They all looked at the shelves above the milk cans. Except for three jars of Recipe in the corner, they were all bare. Miss Mamie's face darkened. "Now isn't that peculiar."

"What's peculiar, sister?"

"We did buy a-dozen-and-a-half jars Saturday, didn't we?"

"Oh yes, I'm certain we did."

"But there are only three jars left. We couldn't have drunk that many in two days. Or if we did, what happened to the empties?"

"They must be around here somewhere."

Cousin Homer, who was watching the exchange closely, suddenly gave the ladies a sheepish smile. "I . . . uh, must make a small confession, Miss Mamie and Miss Emily. As you observed earlier, Miss Mamie, I'm afraid I am extremely ill suited to this kind of work. A man spends his entire adult life pursuin' the intricate and lofty paths of commerce, and then is stunned to find himself a servile paradigm of clumsiness in the simplest of menial chores."

"Why, whatever in the world are you talken about, Cousin Homer?"

"A most unfortunate accident, I'm afraid, Miss Mamie. While transportin' those new jars from the storeroom to this chamber this mornin', my foot entangled itself with its own counterpart. The result, I fear, was a shattering disintegration of the entire lot of containers."

"Oh dear! You didn't injure yourself, did you, Homer?"

"Not a scratch, dear Emily. A fact which served only to amplify my chagrin and mortification."

"Oh, it's not important, Cousin Homer," Miss Emily soothed. "You mustn't feel bad."

"Certainly not," Miss Mamie chimed in. "We'll have twelve dozen tomorrow. Now you just stop worryen yourself about it. Eighteen empty jars just don't mean one thing!"

Jenny was staring at Cousin Homer, amazed by his performance. He smiled sadly at the two sisters and slowly shook his head.

"Ladies, your beauty and charm is surpassed only by your infinite generosity."

"Oh, now, go along with you, Cousin Homer." Miss Emily giggled. "What we have to do now is get this next batch straightened out before it all turns to sugar candy. That happened once before, years ago. Remember, Mamie?"

"Oh my, yes. We were havin' company, and just

havin' so much fun we got the ingredients all wrong and then plumb forgot about it cookin' in here. In the mornen the room was three inches deep in hard sugar candy."

"Yes, it took Mr. Crittenbarger two weeks to chop it all out."

"And didn't Mr. Crittenbarger love the Recipe! I think the saddest day of his life was when he finished cleanin' out this room and had to go home."

Cousin Homer Lee was smiling at the ladies and Jenny glanced at John-Boy.

"Well, I guess I'll be choppen that wood and bringen it in for you, Miss Mamie."

"That's fine, John-Boy. And Jenny, you just stay right here. After we get the Recipe properly cooken here, I've got a surprise for you!"

John-Boy gave Jenny a disappointed smile and went outside.

Most of the wood stacked behind the Baldwin sisters' house had been delivered by John Walton late last fall. The logs were cut into short lengths, but still had to be split to be used as stovewood. John-Boy pulled down six chunks and got the ax, wondering if his father ever accepted jars of Recipe in exchange for the wood. If he did he would never dare bring any of them home. They would be emptied into the sink a half second after Olivia sniffed the contents. But there had been occasions, usually after he had gone fishing, when John Walton came home more bright-eyed than usual. And his mood seemed to have no correlation with the size of his catch.

"That's a fine ax you swing there, John-Boy."

The voice gave him a start. John-Boy had heard no doors closing, nor any footsteps, but Cousin Homer Lee was suddenly standing behind him, his thumbs hooked into his suspenders.

"Well, I get a lot of practice at home, Cousin Homer."

"It's a fine thing when a lad helps around the house. I think I can attribute a great measure of my success in the business world to the simple virtues I learned doin' chores at home. Hard work builds character."

"Yes, sir." John-Boy nodded. He tossed the split pieces to the side and set up another log.

Cousin Homer moved closer. "Say, John-Boy, I don't want to impinge on your good nature, but I wonder if you might do me another small favor?"

"Sure."

"It's the dear ladies' welfare I have in mind. And frankly, John-Boy, I'm a little worried." Cousin Homer frowned darkly and kicked at the dirt. "One never knows when one gets older. Why, in Chicago last summer I observed a man—couldn't have been forty years of age—grasp at his heart while standin' on a street corner. A minute later, rest his soul, he was dead." Cousin Homer snapped his fingers. "Just like that. Now I'm not suggestin' that either Miss Emily or Miss Mamie is in ill health. Why I wouldn't be surprised if they both lived to be a hundred and ten. But you just never know, John-Boy."

"I expect not."

"But I could never forgive myself, John-Boy, if it were within my power to save one of the dear ladies, and by some oversight, by some lack or preparedness, I found myself unable to do so. What I'm talken about, John-Boy, is a new battery for the Baldwin sisters' vehicle."

"I see," John-Boy said, but he didn't see at all.

"You can imagine if there were an emergency, and I should run out to the car to go for a doctor, and there I should find a dead battery. In those few lost minutes, John-Boy, those precious minutes, I could lose a cousin. And I don't think I have to tell you the high regard with which I hold those dear ladies."

"No sir."

"So, what is our problem? The ladies, it seems, do not feel any urgency about having their automobile ready and able to operate at a moment's notice. It seems that they very seldom use the vehicle and regard its condition with, uh, we might say, indifference."

John-Boy nodded. It was true the Baldwin sisters very seldom drove anywhere.

"Now, the problem, John-Boy, is that I find myself temporarily without ready funds. All my cash, unfortunately, is tied up in foreign banks, trust funds, securities of a various nature, things like that. I'm sure you're familiar with the liquidity problems of high finance. In any case, should it be needed, I deem it essential that medical care be available within minutes for my cousins. The Baldwins, you may not be aware, have a fragile bloodline. And for that reason, John-Boy, a battery must be secured for their car with the utmost haste."

"I really don't have any money to be lenden you, Cousin Homer."

"Ah, dear boy, such an imposition on our short friendship would never enter my mind. 'Neither a lender nor a borrower be' has been my constant and unswerving financial credo. No, what I'm askin', John-Boy, is a far simpler thing. I want you to do no more than secure a new battery from Mr. Ike Godsey, whom I understand is the proprietor of the local mercantile establishment, and charge it to the account of the Baldwin sisters. This is something I would never consider, John-Boy, unless I were convinced that it was necessary for their own health and welfare. And have no fear, there is every indication that my financial position will become far more liquid in the near future. At that time I will personally settle the bill with Mr. Godsey, and the battery will thus become a gift from me to my dear cousins, and will be given with my blessin's and best wishes. However, in order for me to attend to my affairs—sign papers, consult with my bankers, that sort of thing—I shall be required to journey into Charlottesville and perhaps Richmond. I am sure you can appreciate that, John-Boy."

John-Boy nodded. He saw no reason for Cousin Homer circling around the tree ten or twelve times before he made the request to charge the car battery. Miss Emily and Miss Mamie probably wouldn't give it a second thought. But John-Boy did see the reason why Homer was so concerned about making trips to Charlottesville and having a car ready to go at a moment's notice. Dependable transportation would be very handy if Sheriff Bridges came looking for him.

"I'm not sure Ike Godsey has any batteries at the store," John-Boy said.

Cousin Homer's face darkened. "Ahhh, that possibility I failed to consider. However, I'm sure you could have him order it. Or better still, if you could drive to Charlottesville in your truck?"

"I don't think I could do that. And I don't expect the Baldwin sisters have credit accounts down there."

"Yes, I see your point. Well, I would greatly appreciate it, John-Boy, if you would have Mr. Godsey take care of the matter as hastily as possible. And have no doubt, my boy, in the endeavor there will be a small gratuity for your services. Say, five dollars if the battery is here within the next two days?"

"That won't be necessary, Cousin Homer." His mother was disturbed enough without his taking money from a bootlegger.

"You're a fine lad, John-Boy. And by the way, you might increase the order for mason jars by another six dozen. I had no idea the ladies were goin' to send out so many invitations."

After Cousin Homer left, John-Boy chopped the rest of the wood, wondering if he should report the conversation to Sheriff Bridges. With a new battery in the Baldwin sisters' car, Homer just might load up with Recipe and disappear in the middle of the night. And the theft of all the Recipe would probably be disastrous for the ladies' family reunion.

John-Boy carried the wood inside and found Miss Mamie and Miss Emily in the parlor. But just inside the door he stopped short and caught his breath.

Standing in the middle of the room, Jenny Pendleton was wearing a long hoopskirted dress covered with yellow ribbons. In her hand she had a matching parasol, and a huge picture hat extended below her shoulders. John-Boy had seen pictures of southern belles in the Civil War era, but none of them looked so beautiful as Jenny.

The Baldwin sisters were smiling with delight, and Jenny twirled lightly around, revealing some kind of ruffled pantaloons on her legs.

"You like it, John-Boy?"

"Yes," he choked.

"Doesn't she look just lovely," Miss Emily sighed. "That's the dress I was wearen when Ashley Longworth kissed me under the maple tree."

"And our grandmother wore it at a reception for General Robert E. Lee almost seventy-five years ago."

"And we want Jenny to wear it at our family reunion!"

Jenny blushed and looked helplessly at John-Boy. The dress was beautiful, but not exactly the kind of thing young girls wore these days.

"It's sure the prettiest dress I ever saw," John-Boy said.

"And we think Jenny is the prettiest girl in all of Walton's Mountain, and that she should wear it. Don't you agree, John-Boy?"

"If Ashley Longworth is coming," Jenny said, "I think you should wear the dress, Miss Emily."

Miss Emily smiled shyly and gave her sister a cautious glance. "Oh, I don't think Ashley would remember. And the dress is for someone young and gay. For someone who's expecten to be courted."

"I think the dress would look real nice on you, Miss Emily."

"Do you really think so, John-Boy?"

Miss Mamie was gazing wistfully at the dress as if her thoughts were on the happier days of grand parties and handsome young men. She took a long breath and looked firmly at Emily. "Sister," she said with sudden decisiveness, "I agree with Jenny and John-Boy. *You* should wear the dress."

Miss Emily gasped and then looked hesitantly at each of them, as if to reassure herself of their sincerity. They were all smiling, waiting for her decision.

"Well," she murmured, "I ... I suppose I could wear it. I mean, if y'all really think ..." Her eyes suddenly glistened and she fumbled for a handkerchief. "I just don't know. I mean if ... I'm just not sure it still fits."

"Of course it'll fit." Miss Mamie smiled. "And you'll look lovelier than ever in it!"

Miss Emily blew hard into the handkerchief. But she still had trouble getting words out. "You'll all just ... have to excuse me." She laughed weakly. "I just don't know what's come over me all of a sudden. It's just the strangest thing ..." She suddenly rose and hurried from the room.

Ike Godsey was busy with two other customers when John-Boy brought in the invitations for mailing. Mrs. Merrill was at the counter, placing her purchases in a basket while Ike toted up her bill, and the other woman, Mrs. Latham, was at the rear. John-Boy's attention went immediately to Mrs. Latham.

Clay Latham was one of the few people in Walton's Mountain who had a regular job. He had once been a foreman at the soapstone plant down in Charlottesville, but since so many men had been laid off he now operated a cutting machine. But he had a steady check coming in every week, and what alarmed John-Boy was that Mrs. Latham was now gazing thoughtfully at the used washing machine in the back corner. John-Boy set the envelopes in front of Ike's post-office cage and hurried back.

"Hello, John-Boy." Mrs. Latham smiled.

John-Boy nodded. "Mrs. Latham."

Once he was at her side, John-Boy didn't know exactly what to do. Mrs. Latham touched the wringer mechanism, ran her fingers along the rollers, and drew back her hand.

"That's a right old machine, Mrs. Latham. Second-hand, you know."

"Not many people can afford new ones these days, John-Boy."

"I expect so, but sometimes buyen old ones costs more fixen 'em up than new ones'd cost."

"Yes. But Clay's very good at fixin' things."

"If you can get parts. Sometimes the right parts are hard to find."

Mrs. Latham nodded vaguely and lifted the lid from the tub. "Well," she sighed and replaced it, "I expect I'd better talk to Clay 'bout it first. Nice-looken machine, though."

To John-Boy's relief she smiled at him and moved away. Mrs. Merrill was finished at the counter and the two women went out the door together.

"What can I do for you, John-Boy?"

"I'd sure appreciate it, Ike, if you'd put a sign on that machine sayen it's sold."

Ike laughed. "There's a slight difference between sold and a down payment, John-Boy."

John-Boy pulled a wad of crumpled bills from his pocket. "Look-a-here, Ike. Five more dollars to add to the dollar I already paid."

"Fine. And I'll give you a receipt. Nineteen more dollars and I'll put a sold sign on it."

"Fourteen more, Ike. The price was twenty dollars."

"Was it twenty? Yep, I guess you're right. You're a sharp trader, John-Boy."

"And I want a hundred and twenty-seven three-cent stamps." John-Boy brought out three dollars and eighty-one cents from another pocket.

"Go 'long." Ike glanced at the envelopes. "Whatcha got over there? You startin' one o' them chain letters or somethin'?"

"They're for the Baldwin sisters' reunion. They've invited every Baldwin in the country."

"Okay, I'll get you the stamps. But I just sell 'em, John-Boy, I don't lick 'em. And the mason jars is in. You wanta take 'em with you?"

"I'll get 'em in the mornen. And there's somethin' else. Cousin Homer Lee wants me to pick up another six dozen jars. And do you have a battery that'll fit the Baldwin sisters' car?"

"Sure do. They ask you to pick one up?"

"Well, not exactly. Cousin Homer Lee wants it."

Ike nodded. "Cousin Homer wants it, eh? He give you the money for the extra jars and the battery?"

"No. He wants 'em charged to the Baldwins' account."

"I see." Ike frowned and carefully counted stamps. "John-Boy, it don't make no difference to me about chargin' more jars and a battery to the Baldwins. I know they'll pay. But knowin' what I know, I got a feelin' Ep Bridges might wanta know about them extra jars. And he might not be too partial to the idea of the Baldwin sisters' car bein' in good operatin' condition. What d'ya think?"

John-Boy smiled. "I was kinda thinken the same thing. Will you tell the Sheriff?"

"Glad to. He oughta be in for a game of pool pretty soon. He might like the idea of keepen Cousin Homer Lee bottled up out there for a while with no transportation. I'll let you know what he says in the mornin'."

On the way home John-Boy made a slight detour past Jenny's house. He'd said good night to her earlier, when they walked home from the Baldwins. But he already missed her.

For several minutes he stood in front of the house, watching, seeing nothing behind the closed curtains. But knowing she was inside was enough. He finally smiled and turned away.

"Hey, John-Boy." His father smiled when he got home. "We gonna have the honor of your company for supper tonight?"

John-Boy laughed, realizing he had been late or missed supper entirely for the last three days. His father was heading for the barn to milk the cow.

"You want me to do that for you, Daddy?"

"Be glad for your company."

John-Boy got the milking stool and waited until his father poured some mash in the feeding trough. Chance had strong opinions about people paying for her services. No food in the trough meant no messing around with her milk supply.

"You ever see such a fine day as today?" John-Boy asked idly.

John Walton gave the boy an amused glance. He didn't remember John-Boy ever taking much interest in the weather before. "It was uncommonly pretty. Looks like spring is here to stay."

"I reckon spring is about my favorite season of the year, Daddy."

"It's a fair time."

After he finished pouring mash, John leaned on the

railing and watched the boy milk the cow. The dreamy look in John-Boy's eyes suggested he was thinking about more than the weather.

"Daddy?"

"Yes, son?"

"You ever been in love?"

"Yep. Still am."

"How'd you know it was love? I mean, when it first hit you."

"Scared me to death."

John-Boy gaped at him. "Scared you to death?"

"Scared me that maybe she didn't feel the same way."

"How was that?"

"The way it still is. The first face that comes into my mind when I wake in the mornen. The face I carry into sleep each night. A feelen that never stops of needen her, and bein' needed."

John-Boy's face brightened. "Lordee, don't I know!"

"You and Jenny, huh?"

John-Boy turned back to his work, blushing. "You like her, Daddy?"

"She's a sweet little girl."

"You think Mama likes her?"

"I can't see any reason why not."

John-Boy seemed satisfied with that. "Jenny loves it here," he said after a minute. "She says you and Mama are the finest people she ever met. She says she could just hug Elizabeth to pieces."

John Walton smiled. "I think you got about all you're goen to get outa that cow, John-Boy."

Chance had twisted her head, glaring at John-Boy, apparently having the same thought.

VIII

John-Boy had not expected his euphoric relationship with Jenny to become the topic of discussion at the Walton supper table—at least not ten minutes after he had revealed the secret to his father. But as quickly as he washed his hands and came to the table, he sat down before an audience of hushed, staring faces. Some were smiling, others gaped openly, while his mother and father, it seemed, were doing their best to avoid showing any expression at all.

"What's the matter?" John-Boy asked as the food was passed.

That triggered suppressed laughter from Mary Ellen and Ben. Then the other children joined in.

"Why you all laughen? Somebody swallow some giggle water?"

Apparently this was funnier yet, and Erin could hold it no longer. As if it were the most incredible thing in the world, she asked, "Are you in love, John-Boy?"

"Daddy said you were," Jim-Bob grinned.

"Daddy said you've really got it bad," Jason added. "Is it true, John-Boy?"

"Now, children," Olivia cautioned.

And then Elizabeth broke the tension, even bringing a smile to John-Boy's reddening face. With a look of awed concern she asked, "Does it hurt, John-Boy?"

Until that moment John-Boy had a feeling of being betrayed. His father must have made the announcement the minute he sat down at the table. But there was no sign of ridicule in the circle of grinning faces. Grandpa was beaming, his mother and father were smiling sympathetically, and the others had looks of wonder or curious interest. Mostly, John-Boy guessed, he was glad the secret was out. Still he felt he had to play the game.

"What'd you have to go and tell everybody for, Daddy?"

His father's grin indicated he had no regrets about what he had done. "Why, John-Boy, when two young people fall in love, I don't see why it ought to be a secret. Seems to me instead of whisperen it, somebody ought to shoot off Roman candles or sing a Hallelujah chorus! Don't you think so, Grandpa?"

"Ought to be dancen on the rooftops, I'd say!"

"Well," Grandma sighed, "you two can sing Hallelujah choruses and dance on the roof if you want. I'm goen to eat my supper!"

"Old woman," Grandpa challenged, "where's your spirit of romance?"

"Hah! Look who's talken! When was the last time you kissed me?"

The pressure was clearly off of him now, and John-Boy smiled. Then they all laughed as Grandpa promptly responded. He put an arm around her, pulled her close, and planted a big kiss on her mouth.

"You old fool!" she said and pulled herself away. "Now, will someone please pass the gravy?"

The next two days were a glorious time for John-Boy. He and Jenny took another hike to the mountain and discovered new meadows and springs and shaded glens. And they discovered each other.

Jenny told him about her life in St. Petersburg and the terrible feelings of fear and emptiness she had experienced after her mother's death. She and her father had become very close after that, and when Eula came along Jenny hated her and resented every minute she took of her father's time. The remarkable thing about it, Jenny observed now, was how kind and patient Eula had been through it all. It was Eula, more than her father, who insisted that Jenny participate in everything they did. And while Jenny did everything in her power to break up the relationship, Eula responded only with love and kindness. It must have been terrible for her father. And when they finally married, Jenny's running away was more of a gift to them than it was an act of anger or frustration. She was ashamed of her behavior during the previous year and thought there was nothing better she could give them for a wedding present than some time to themselves. But even that, she now realized, was foolish.

However, that was all in the past. They were a family now, and they could talk and laugh about the silly things all of them had done through that difficult time. Jenny and Eula seemed to grow closer every day, and Jenny could no longer imagine a life without her new stepmother.

John-Boy told her about his hopes of going to college and becoming a writer. He was not certain how either of these dreams was going to be transformed into reality, but there was no doubt in either of their minds that the obstacles would be overcome. While they sat by a bubbling spring or lay back and closed their eyes to the burning sun, John-Boy talked about travels to Tasmania and Fiji and Micronesia, and Jenny suggested that when they went to bed each night all of their children would call out "Good night" to each other. They would see Barcelona and Istanbul and Athens, John-Boy reflected, and Jenny said she would cook and clean and care for their children the way John-Boy's mother did. And while John-Boy was writing his books the whole family would sit and watch his face and be completely silent.

They marveled at the fact that only a few days before neither of them even knew the other existed. But now their love for each other was the most enduring thing in each of their lives.

The night after John-Boy's affliction was announced at the supper table, Mary Ellen's dreams of riches as America's foremost supplier of frogs' legs almost came to an abrupt end. It was only due to Reckless's alert vigilance that disaster was averted.

Mary Ellen's suspicions had been aroused the previous day when her carefully calculated inventory of polliwogs revealed an alarming discrepancy. Through a twenty-four-hour period the embryonic amphibians wiggling about in her four backyard pools diminished in number by at least fifty; or as Mary Ellen viewed it, by at least one hundred fat and succulent and very valuable frogs' legs. There were no lifeless bodies in the pools to indicate they had died from natural causes, nor were any of them developed enough to leave the water under their own power. Mary Ellen's immediate suspicions fell on Erin.

"The last thing in the world I would ever do," Erin haughtily informed her, "would be to go within one hundred feet of those dirty little creatures."

"You were standen right next to the pool yesterday," Jim-Bob pointed out heatedly.

The confrontation took place in the girls' bedroom where Erin was quietly brushing her hair. Mary Ellen had brought along Ben, Jim-Bob, and Elizabeth to serve as both reinforcements and witnesses.

"It was a mean thing to do," Elizabeth said, "and we're goen to tell Mama."

"I haven't the slightest idea what you're all talkin' about," Erin sighed, "and furthermore, I couldn't care less."

"What did you do with them?" Mary Ellen demanded.

"Would you all please leave my room?"

"It's our room just as much as it is yours," Elizabeth informed her.

"That's right," Mary Ellen agreed. "And we're warnen you right now, Erin, we're goen to watch you every minute of the day from now on."

"Well, I don't think you'll find it very exciting."

That afternoon the four partners captured enough replacements to bring the inventory back to normal, but there was no doubt in their minds that Erin was plotting desperately to sabotage the project. While Mary Ellen and Elizabeth went for more polliwogs Jim-Bob and Ben stood guard over the pools, and through the remainder of the day there was not a minute during which at least one of them didn't have the area under careful surveillance. By suppertime they agreed that the danger had passed and they had only to keep a watchful eye out for the possibility of Erin slipping outside unnoticed. This presented no difficulties while Erin and Mary Ellen did the dishes.

"Did you find your dumb polliwogs?" Erin asked.

"It's none of your business," Mary Ellen countered, "but we're goen to have plenty of them."

"I'd just as soon eat a worm as a frog."

"Then you're not a goor-met."

"What's a goor-met?"

The question took Mary Ellen by surprise, but she easily handled it. "I don't know. But E. P. Fairweather says they're just crazy about frogs' legs."

"Hmph! I think they're just plain crazy."

"Well, it doesn't make the slightest difference to me if they're crazy or not. It just happens that goor-mets happen to be rich and they happen to like frogs' legs. If they liked worms, I'd sell them a million dollars worth of worms."

"I'll bet you would," Erin said with revulsion.

Mary Ellen had no chance to respond. Outside the kitchen window Reckless exploded into a fury of yelping and whining as if he had been attacked by an army of cats.

Their father came into the kitchen and quickly peered out the window. "What's goen on?"

"I don't know, Daddy. We didn't hear anythin'."

Reckless sounded hysterical now, and John headed for the door. "Well, it pays to check sometimes. It makes Reckless think he's doen a good job of doggin' if we show him we take it seriously."

Outside, Reckless was still carrying on, leaping against his rope, barking at something off in the darkness.

"S'matter with you, boy?"

Once out the door, Mary Ellen's eyes went directly to the ponds, and then she gasped. There, staring indignantly back at her, were the white-masked eyes of a raccoon. In his curled paw he held a squirming polliwog, which he casually plopped into his mouth.

"Looks like somebody's helpen himself to your polliwogs, Mary Ellen."

In her fury, Mary Ellen picked up the first thing at hand, which turned out to be a hoe. But before she could get to the raccoon, Erin marched past her, swinging the kitchen broom. "Go on, git," she was shouting, "git on out of here!"

"You dirty, thievin' little bandit!" Mary Ellen screamed, following after her. "Get away from my frogs!"

The animal moved with resentful slowness until Erin's broom caught it squarely on the rump. Then it scampered away into the bushes.

"You want bullfrog legs," Mary Ellen shouted after it, "you go down to the creek and collect 'em yourself!"

Reckless was whimpering now, pleading for release to join the chase, but John held him by the collar. "Calm down, Mary Ellen." He laughed. "That ol' raccoon had no way of knowen those bullfrogs belonged to you."

Erin came back with the broom. "More'n likely he'll be right back," she said matter-of-factly.

"Well if he does, he's gonna find me waiten. Can I borrow your shotgun, Daddy?" She stationed herself defiantly between the ponds and the bushes.

In all the excitement, the fact that Erin came to the rescue and drove the raccoon off did not register completely in Mary Ellen's mind until she had been standing guard for some time that night. Her most immediate thoughts were on the danger posed by the hungry animal waiting somewhere out in the darkness. Her father did not permit her to have his shotgun, which might have put a prompt end to the threat. Instead, Mary Ellen sat cross-legged with her back to the ponds and the hoe at her side.

Erin's behavior was very strange, she thought as she reflected on it. It seemed like the thing her sister wanted most in the world was to get rid of all the tadpoles as fast as possible. And yet when they were attacked she came rushing out to protect them with a broom. It didn't make sense. But Mary Ellen quickly shrugged it off. The fact was, most people she knew didn't make a whole lot of sense.

Like John-Boy, for example. Now why, all of a sudden, had he fallen in love with Jenny Pendleton? Jenny appeared to be a perfectly nice girl, and she was pretty and all that. But as far as Mary Ellen could see she wasn't that much different from a dozen other girls around Walton's Mountain.

So why all the magic baloney and John-Boy blushing and carrying on? One day he was perfectly normal, and twenty-four hours later he was all dopey and wandering around like his feet didn't even touch the ground. Such silliness was beyond the realm of Mary Ellen's understanding.

To her it seemed that boys ought to be more interested in whether or not a girl had some good sense rather than if she had pretty eyes or shiny hair. But that, of course, assumed that boys had good sense themselves—an extremely doubtful proposition, from what she had observed.

The screen door banged and Mary Ellen glanced quickly over her shoulder. It was Erin, with a blanket in her hand.

"Daddy told me to bring you this."

"Thanks."

"You goen to stay out here all night?"

"Yes."

Mary Ellen arranged the blanket around her shoulders and glanced up at Erin. She couldn't see her face, but Erin was standing with her arms folded as if waiting for something. Mary Ellen had an idea what it was.

"Thanks for chasen the coon away," she said.

"You're welcome."

Erin still didn't go away.

"And I'm sorry we accused you of takin' the tadpoles."

"You needn't apologize."

"I want to apologize. We were wrong and I'm sorry."

"It isn't necessary."

Mary Ellen felt the back of her neck grow warm. Erin was up on her horse again, acting like the Queen of Sheba.

"All right then, I take back the apology."

"The only thing I wish you'd do, Mary Ellen, is to withhold your judgments and not accuse people of things until you are certain of their guilt."

Mary Ellen bit her tongue. "All right," she said in a measured tone. "But if you hate tadpoles so much, how come you chased the coon away?"

"Because I hate raccoons as much as I hate tadpoles. They're both dirty and despicable."

Mary Ellen pulled the blanket higher around her neck and gazed into the brush, signaling an end to the conversation. It was a pure waste of time talking with stupid people.

"On the other hand," Erin said, turning airily away, "I wouldn't like to see you and the other children disappointed."

Mary Ellen watched her go back to the house and disappear inside, then sighed with resignation.

There was a perfect example of what she had been thinking about earlier. Erin would brush her hair every night for the next five years, and then some boy would go gaga over her. Then he would spend the rest of his life listening to her stupid conversation.

In about two weeks, Mary Ellen consoled herself, there would be about six hundred pairs of fat frogs' legs jumping around in the pools behind her. Then the money would start rolling in, and she would no longer have to put up with all this nonsense.

Sheriff Bridges had done some thinking about Cousin Homer Lee's request for a new battery. The idea of Cousin Homer Lee not having any kind of transportation available appealed to him very much. From the description of Homer Lee Baldwin he had received from the Richmond police department, it didn't seem likely the man would hoist anything onto his shoulder and hike down to Richmond with it. Homer was not a violent criminal type, and he seemed to go to great lengths not to inflict any kind of violence on his own body. And he clearly regarded physical labor as a form of violence to be avoided.

On the other hand, if the lack of a vehicle confined Homer to the Baldwin residence, there would be no opportunity for Ep to catch him in the act of transporting or selling bootleg whiskey It was a knotty problem, to which Ep addressed himself through four pool games with Ike Godsey, and then through several more hours of thoughtful rocking on his own front porch. By the time John-Boy arrived at Ike's store the next morning Ep was back at the pool table, his solution all worked out.

"You go on and take them extra jars, John-Boy. But we'll let Cousin Homer Lee stew for a while over his battery. When are the Baldwin sisters figuren to have that big reunion of theirs?"

"The invitations all said Saturday, startin' about four o'clock."

"That's just fine. You tell Cousin Homer that Ike's orderin' the battery from Richmond, and it'll be here for sure at noon on Saturday. You got that?"

"Yes sir."

"You gonna let him have it?" Ike asked.

Ep Bridges was not above injecting a little drama into his police work. Nor did he mind giving the impression that there was a superior intelligence at work when he was performing his duties. He took his time with a pool shot and studied the balls again.

"It's all in the timin', Ike."

"I don't follow. You give him a battery at noon on Saturday and he's gonna be long gone into the night."

Ep smiled. "That's right. But if he gets that battery

at noon, then I'll know exactly when he'll be leaven, and I'll be waiten."

Ep let the statement hang for a while before he went on. "You all just think on it a minute," he finally said. "All them relatives of the Baldwins is goen to be showen up around four o'clock on Saturday afternoon. Now you just picture Cousin Homer sitten there in that house with a couple hundred jars of Recipe, and him knowen all them relatives is on their way. You can just bet your life that old swindler's not gonna let them uncles and nephews and cousins get their hands on them jars. Noooo, sireee. If that battery's comen at noon, and them relatives is comen at four, Cousin Homer's gonna have that car loaded and out of there as fast as he can. And between noon and four o'clock Sheriff Ep Bridges is gonna be waiten with open arms about a mile down the road."

Ike smiled and nodded his approval.

"So, John-Boy," Ep said, "you just tell ol' Cousin Homer not to worry about a thing. That battery's gonna be there at twelve o'clock sharp without fail."

John-Boy didn't give a lot of thought to Ep Bridges's scheme. More than twelve hours had passed since he had seen Jenny and he wanted only to deliver the new jars and get his work done at the Baldwins' as fast as possible. With love on his mind it didn't make much difference to him if Cousin Homer took every ounce of whiskey in Virginia and ran off to California with it. But Cousin Homer was shocked by the news.

"Saturday! Did you say Saturday, John-Boy?"

John-Boy had never seen Homer move so fast. The minute he arrived at the Baldwins' and started backing the truck up to the garage, Cousin Homer was out the front door and hustling over to him.

"That's what Ike said. He had to call down to Charlottesville and they told him it'd be here around noon Saturday."

"But that's four days off, John-Boy! That's the day of the reunion. Noon, did you say?"

"But I got the extra jars. They're all in the back of the truck."

"The extra jars?"

Homer seemed lost in thought for a minute, but then followed John-Boy to the back of the truck. "Oh, yes, the extra jars. That's fine, John-Boy. Let me give you a hand there."

After the jars were unloaded John-Boy reported to the Baldwin sisters and they set him to work washing the outsides of all the windows. He saw Cousin Homer only once more during the day, and the old man seemed to have regained his composure.

"You're doin' a fine job there, John-Boy. I've always said there's nothin' like plain old soap and elbow grease for gettin' windows clean."

"They're haven me use vinegar, Mr. Baldwin."

"Ah, yes, of course. And nothin' like vinegar for the sparkle."

Cousin Homer had changed into clean white pants and was wearing a hat and coat now. He gave all the windows an approving glance and smiled again. "Say, John-Boy, a thought has been passin' through my mind this mornin'. The germination of an idea, you might say. It occurs to me that in honor of the comen festive occasion; that is, the reunion celebration of my dear cousins next Saturday, it strikes me that perhaps an appropriate gesture on my part might be the purchase of a small gift for the dear ladies. Just a token, mind you, a memento of sorts signifying my affection along with my gratitude for their gracious hospitality."

"I'm sure they'd appreciate that, Cousin Homer."

"Indeed, indeed. And to discharge this familial obligation, I am sure you can understand, John-Boy, that I shall be required to make a short visit to one of the emporiums of Charlottesville. The purchase of an appropriate gift would take but a minute, and I should be back in Walton's Mountain even before my absence is noted. And upon my return, John-Boy, you would find the fuel tank of your father's vehicle filled to capacity."

John-Boy moved to the final window. "I'm sorry, Cousin Homer, but I can't let you use the truck."

"As I explained, John-Boy, there is no thought of *my* using the vehicle. It is to be used solely in the pursuit of a charitable act. Surely you wouldn't deny a small pleasure to those dear ladies who have so graciously provided you with employment?"

If he hadn't been fully aware of what Cousin Homer was up to, John-Boy would have found the appeal hard to refuse. But Sheriff Bridges wouldn't take kindly to his letting Homer drive off to Charlottesville.

"I'm really sorry, Cousin Homer, but I'm gonna be through here in a minute, and my Daddy's expectin' to have the truck back right after lunch. I just can't do it."

Cousin Homer gazed narrowly at him for a minute, then studied the distant hills.

"I'll tell you what I *can* do." John-Boy smiled. "Ike Godsey's got some real nice things down at his general merchandise store. I can drive you down there when I go home."

"Ike Godsey's?" Homer murmured. "No, I'm afraid that would not be suitable for the, uh . . . gift I had in mind."

Cousin Homer moved casually away. John-Boy watched the old man gaze at the empty truck for a while, and then disappear into the Recipe room.

IX

Eating supper at the Pendletons' house was much more formal than at the Waltons'. For one thing there were only four of them, which made the gathering a lot quieter. And another, instead of a big table standing in the middle of the kitchen, the Pendletons had a separate room for the exclusive purpose of eating.

John-Boy's only previous visit to the inside of the house had been the night he and his father entered in search of ghosts. He was amazed by the transformation. Instead of cobwebs and dust and sheet-covered furniture, everything now glistened with polish and had the scent of fresh cut roses and carnations. The tablecloth before him was pure white linen and there was an incredible array of sparkling glasses and silverware.

Olivia had insisted that John-Boy wear his best Sunday clothes for the occasion. She had used a damp cloth to press his pants, and Grandma had carefully inspected his shirt and stitched over the worst of the threadbare spots.

"Don't see why you're all maken so much fuss about his eatin' at Dave Pendleton's," his father shrugged. "Dave's lived in Walton's Mountain long enough to know we don't act like city people."

No one responded to the observation. Even the other children seemed to understand that there was something very important about John-Boy's invitation to supper. While he was not expected to ask formally for Jenny's hand in marriage, or undergo any cross-examination from Dave Pendleton, there was still the need for some kind of approval. Fathers have ambitions for their daughters. And what did Eula Pendleton, who'd probably spent all her life in the refined society of city life, think about her new stepdaughter associating with the son of a rural mountain woodcutter? Whatever she might think, Olivia was determined that there would be no grounds for criticism of John-Boy's cleanliness or manners.

"A gentleman always pulls a chair out for a lady, and never sits down until all the ladies are seated. And if there's more than one fork or spoon, you start with the one's farthest away from the plate. And don't ask for seconds, John-Boy. Always wait until they're offered."

"If there's more than one fork or spoon," Grandpa said, "you bring them extras home, John-Boy."

"Hush up, old man," Grandma said. "A little practice in good manners wouldn't hurt you none."

"Too late for that." Grandpa laughed. "Been shoven food straight in my mouth too long to start learnen how to stick my little finger out while I do it."

If there hadn't been so much fuss over everything at home, John-Boy wouldn't have given a second thought to the evening. But when Jenny breathlessly opened the front door to let him in, he suddenly felt like his arms and legs had all been inserted into the wrong sockets. In her bubbling enthusiasm, Jenny didn't seem to notice the affliction, and she led him into the living room where Dave and Eula were sipping drinks. After half an hour in there they all went to the dining room without John-Boy having uttered more than three words.

Jenny and her stepmother continued into the kitchen for the food, and John-Boy stood awkwardly behind a chair.

"Sit down, John-Boy. They'll be gettin' things ready. Jenny tells me you've been workin' for the Baldwin sisters."

John-Boy sat down. "Yes sir."

"They still makin' that Recipe of old Judge Baldwin's?"

"Yes sir."

Dave Pendleton lit a cigarette and smiled. "I only tasted it once. In fact it was with your dad about fifteen years ago. As I recall we were goin' to look at some land out past the old Crater place, and your dad suggested we make a social call on the Baldwins as long as we were passin' by." He laughed. "And that was the end of that. We never did get past the Baldwins'. About midnight your dad slung me over his shoulder and carried me all the way home. I've often wondered if he really was interested in seein' that land out there."

He laughed again and John-Boy smiled and nodded, not sure what response was expected of him. He appreciated the humor, but he didn't want to seem disrespectful toward his father.

Eula Pendleton came in with a silver tray filled with beef slices and John-Boy quickly came to his feet.

"Sit down, sit down, John-Boy. It'll be a couple minutes yet." She returned to the kitchen and John-Boy sat down.

"Jenny also tells me you're gonna be a writer."

"I'd like to."

"You know, if you're gettin' the impression that Jenny tells me a lot about you, your impression is quite correct. Her principal topic of conversation is John-Boy Walton. Her second topic is the Walton family. And by the time she gets through talkin' about all that, it's usually past midnight and bedtime. In fact, since we've come back to Walton's Mountain I haven't been able to squeeze in two sentences with her."

"Oh, Daddy, that's not true!"

Both Jenny and her mother were bringing food in. John-Boy rose and was relieved when Dave Pendleton also came to his feet. They seated the ladies and returned to their chairs.

Dave Pendleton bowed his head. "Lord, we thank you for this food, and we especially thank you for John-Boy Walton's presence. Now we won't have to listen to Jenny talk about him anymore. Amen."

"Oh, Daddy, what kind of a prayer is that?"

"Right from the heart, Jenny."

Through the meal Dave Pendleton's relaxed humor helped ease John-Boy's tensions. And the happy smiles he got from Jenny were like rays of glorious sunshine. Eula Pendleton was as quiet as John-Boy, and appeared content to let her husband do the talking while she saw that everyone's plate was full. After dessert Dave Pendleton pushed back his chair and grinned.

"John-Boy, while the servants here clean up the dishes, let's you and me go out on the porch and get some air."

"That's not fair, Daddy," Jenny protested.

"What do you mean it's not fair? I think it's my turn now. After he goes home I can come into your room and talk and talk all night about what a wonderful young man he is. And you can listen for a change. Come on, John-Boy."

John-Boy would rather have stayed in the house within sight of Jenny, but there seemed to be no choice. Jenny made a face at her father and then hurried out of range from his playful swing at her rear.

Once they were on the porch Dave Pendleton stretched and looked around at the sky and the distant mountains before he sat down. "I think this is what I missed most livin' in the city. Just sittin' on a porch with nothin' around but mountains and stars and crickets. It's beautiful here, isn't it, John-Boy."

"Yes, it's nice and quiet," John-Boy agreed. But he sometimes wondered if the bustle of activity in the city might not be more interesting.

After a couple minutes of silence, Dave Pendleton looked off at the hills and smiled reflectively. "You know somethin', John-Boy, the first time I was ever courtin' seriously enough to go to a girl's house for dinner it turned out to be the most embarrassing

experience of my entire life." He shook his head and
chuckled to himself. "My mother told me one of the
most important things was to be sure and tilt the soup
bowl toward myself instead of away, toward the center
of the table. Well, I was so nervous about doin' everythin' just right, I forgot that it wasn't necessary to tip
the soup bowl at all until I got down to the last drop of
the stuff. So the minute the soup was served I reached
for the bowl and tipped it."

John-Boy smiled, picturing hot soup pouring onto
the table. But Dave Pendleton held up his hand.

"Don't laugh. That was embarrassing enough, but
that was just the beginning, John-Boy. The soup was
scaldin' hot, and it landed right in my lap. Well, you
can imagine how I was a little anxious to stand up and
get rid of the stuff as fast as I could. Well, that's what I
did, and I think I broke a world's record for anyone
gettin' on his feet. I'd say I accomplished it in just
about the same instant the soup hit my pants.

"Well, it was fast, but the unfortunate thing was the
direction of the movement was very poorly calculated.
As quickly as I stood up, I also lifted my side of the table about a foot off the floor. And that action immediately put everyone else at the table into the same predicament I was in a half second earlier."

Dave Pendleton shook his head sadly, and John-Boy
couldn't help laughing. It was easy for him to imagine
himself in the same predicament.

Dave Pendleton started to go on, but then he too
started laughing. When he finally caught his breath
there were tears streaming down his face. "Somehow, I
don't think the girl's mother and father were much im-
pressed by my apologies. I think I said I was sorry
about forty times—about twenty times while I followed
them all to the bathroom, and then twenty more times
after they went inside and slammed the door in my
face."

The picture of the whole family locked in a
bathroom and a sixteen-year-old boy calling apologies
through the door sent them both into another paroxysm
of laughter.

"I'm tellin' you, John-Boy," Dave said through his

tears, "it was the damnedest experience I ever had in my life. That was the first time I ever heard an adult woman swear like a coal miner. All dressed up like the Queen of England . . . with soup running down and dripping over her shoes . . . and the damnedest words you ever heard comin' out of her mouth. John-Boy, some of those words I've never heard since."

After another half minute of laughter, he said, "And the father couldn't get a word out. I kept sayin' I was sorry, and he just stared at me, openin' and closin' his mouth. For a minute I thought he was havin' a heart attack."

He shook his head again, as if unable to believe his own story. "I waited around outside the bathroom for about half an hour, but they never came out. So I went home." He laughed again. "I never saw the girl again. The whole family moved away about two weeks later. I don't think any of 'em came out of the house durin' that whole two weeks. Maybe they never even came out of the bathroom."

John-Boy didn't realize he had been laughing so hard. That was the end of the story, but they both sat for several minutes, catching their breath. "I think I know how you felt," John-Boy finally said.

"Well, mothers are great," Dave Pendleton smiled. "But sometimes they can get you in all kinds of trouble." He took a deep breath and let it out with a final laugh.

"You know, John-Boy, it's funny bein' a father of a daughter. You worry yourself sick wonderin' if the poor girl is ever goin' to have any boyfriends. Then the first one starts hangin' around and you start worryin' about too many of 'em showin' up. Or you worry about her pickin' the wrong one. And then you start worryin' about your worryin'." He laughed and closed his eyes. "John-Boy, your father is the finest man I know on this entire earth. And your family's the best people I know. And I just can't tell you how happy I am about you and Jenny hittin' it off the way you have. I don't think there's anythin' in the world that could make me any happier than I am right now."

John-Boy felt his skin flush from the top of his head

down to his toes. He knew Dave Pendelton told him the story about the soup to put him at ease, and he appreciated it. But he never expected him to say anything like he had just said.

"That's real nice of you to say that, Mr. Pendelton. And I expect I'd say the same thing about you and Mrs. Pendelton. And about Jenny, of course." He felt his throat thickening. "And I expect right now I'm just about as happy as you are."

Dave Pendelton smiled warmly at him. "Well, I guess that takes care of our obligations to have a heart-to-heart talk, young man." He gave John-Boy a look of mock severity. "I judge from your statements, sir, that your intentions are honorable, and you intend to provide for my daughter in a manner suitable to her station in life?"

"I do, sir." John-Boy smiled.

"Very well, sir. Then I think it is time to join the ladies."

They both rose, but at that moment Jenny and Eula came out the door.

"What in the world have you two been laughin' and gigglin' about?"

"Strictly gentlemen's talk, Eula dear. John-Boy and I have been discussin' business affairs and the state of the world. And the incredibly high price one can pay for a bowl of soup these days."

Both of the men laughed, which brought suspicious frowns from Eula and Jenny.

"Well, I don't expect we'll ever find out what that's all about." Eula smiled. "Do you have any cigarettes, Dave?"

He searched his pockets. "By golly, I don't. I meant to buy some today over at Ike's. Well, that gives us a good excuse to go for a drive over to Charlottesville and leave these two kids alone. Do you think we can trust 'em?"

"That's not very complimentary to John-Boy."

Dave winked at his daughter and grinned. "It's not John-Boy I'm worried about. It's been my experience that the female of the species is far more likely to be the predator."

After they drove off, John-Boy and Jenny sat quietly on the porch swing for a long time. Jenny rested her head on his shoulder, and John-Boy held her, feeling contented and full of love. He felt the same way Dave Pendleton did; that nothing in the world could make him happier than he was at this moment.

"What are you thinking about, John-Boy?"

After a minute he smiled. "I don't think I'm thinken about anythin' at all. It's like bein' on top of a mountain. There's nothin' any higher or any better and I'm just sittin' here breathin' the fresh air and feelin' all the good feelin's."

"I love you, John-Boy."

"I love you, Jenny."

In the long silence that followed, John-Boy marveled at his newfound discoveries about love. It was not really necessary for them to say they loved each other. It was far more clearly communicated through the gentle touch of their hands and the light scent of her hair against his cheek. He felt they could sit here forever and be the happiest people on earth without saying another word to each other. But the sitting part, he knew, was impossible.

"I'd better get goen, Jenny. Daddy wants me to help bring some more logs down in the mornen."

She nodded, but held him for another minute. When they rose John-Boy gave her a lingering kiss, and then another before he left her at the gate.

There was no moon out, and John-Boy walked cautiously along the dirt road toward home. It seemed to be an unusually warm night for this time of year. And he was tired. He had worked hard dragging and loading logs during the day. And there had been all the anxieties through supper at the Pendletons'. And then the laughter, which still ached in his stomach. It had been a long day, and he was ready for bed.

But suddenly and unaccountably, in spite of the warmth, John-Boy felt a chill run down his spine. There seemed to be an eeriness to the night that gave him an uneasy feeling. Warm breezes seemed to rustle the leaves for a moment and then stop, as if some kind of storm were making tentative probes at Walton's Mountain. John-Boy looked curiously at the sky and the surrounding darkness as he walked. But he saw nothing to explain the strange feelings.

Reckless was the only one up to greet him. The old hound whined and whipped his tail and tugged at his rope, and then settled down again as John-Boy went through the back door.

When he reached the top of the stairs his father called from his bedroom. "That you, John-Boy?"

"Yes, Daddy."

"Have a good time?"

"Had a fine time, Daddy."

After a pause there was a smile in his father's voice. "Good night, John-Boy."

"Good night, Daddy."

John-Boy had gotten out of the habit of saying his prayers when he went to bed. But tonight there seemed to be an odd compulsion for him to communicate with some higher power. In solemn tones he said the Lord's Prayer, and then gazed at the ceiling for a long time before he finally went to sleep.

"John-Boy, you'd better get up."

In John-Boy's groggy consciousness the voice was soft and seemed to have an ominous quality. He blinked at the dark figure beside him and quickly looked at the window. There was no sign of light outside.

"Daddy?"

The figure nodded and rose from the bed. "Ep Bridges is down in the kitchen, son. Put somethin' on and come down."

John-Boy stared blankly at the open door as his father quietly left. The Sheriff? His thoughts immediately went to Homer Lee Baldwin, but he knew it was not that. It was something far worse than that. John-Boy held his breath for a minute and then turned on the light and rolled out of bed.

He dressed quickly, telling himself it couldn't be Jenny. She was fine when he left her, and her parents certainly came home minutes after that. But why had the Sheriff come here? And why had his father awakened him? His heart was pounding furiously as he went down the dark stairs.

His mother was standing by the sink, her robe clutched tightly around her. His father stood beside her, and Sheriff Bridges had one arm resting on the top of the refrigerator. They were all grimly silent, apparently waiting for him.

"Sit down, John-Boy," his father said.

John-Boy didn't want to sit down. He stood at the end of the table, glancing from one face to another.

"There's been an accident," Sheriff Bridges said. "Down near Charlottesville. A car ran into Dave Pendleton."

John-Boy took a sharp breath. The fact that Jenny was not involved quickly fled from his mind and he pictured a dark intersection and a sudden violent collision.

"Eula Pendleton was hurt," Sheriff Bridges went on, "but it looks like she'll be all right." He took a long breath and got it over with quickly. "Dave was killed."

John-Boy felt his throat tighten, making it impossible to swallow. His thoughts returned to Jenny. "Did you . . . does Jenny know?"

"That's why Ep came over, son."

Sheriff Bridges nodded. "I went over there right away. I told her as gently as I could. But there ain't no way you can tell a thing like that gentle." He shook his head. "I thought she was goin' to scream for a minute. I wish she had. But she just opened her mouth and closed it. Then she jumped up and ran out the back door."

John-Boy felt his heart drop. "Where'd she go?"

"I don' know, John-Boy. I chased after her, but I couldn't see a thing out back. She must of just kept runnin' full speed. And that's why I came over here. I thought she might of come to your place."

John-Boy looked at his mother and father and knew they had seen nothing of Jenny. Then he pictured her running blindly through the darkness. He had to find her. She needed him more than anything in the world now.

"You know anyplace else she might have gone, John-Boy? Any other friends she might have run to?"

John-Boy shook his head. She would have come to him. Why hadn't she come to him? Had she tried to come, and maybe fell down in the darkness and hurt herself? "I don't know any place, Sheriff. She don't know anybody else around."

Ep Bridges nodded and straightened from the refrigerator. "Well I better get back to lookin' for her then."

"Can I go with him, Daddy?"

"I think it'd be a good idea, son. And maybe I can start worken my way down toward the Pendleton house from here."

The wind was still blowing in short gusts when John-Boy went out to Sheriff Bridges's car. But the balmy warmth was gone now. They rode silently down the road John-Boy had walked two hours earlier, and an agonized feeling of fear and emptiness now gripped him. It seemed impossible that Dave Pendleton could be dead. He was too alive and too happy and too full of love to be gone so suddenly. And Jenny! He couldn't bear to think of her stumbling through the woods somewhere. Oh my God! he thought. She needed him. And he needed to take her in his arms and hold her, and cry with her.

John-Boy was hardly conscious of the car stopping. But he stumbled out and followed the Sheriff into the Pendleton house.

"She might have come back," Ep said.

But the house was empty. John-Boy went from room to room, calling her name, and then did the same upstairs. Sheriff Bridges searched the backyard and came back empty-handed.

"You ain't got no notion of where she might have gone, John-Boy?"

John-Boy shook his head, but then had a remote thought. Could she have gone up on the mountain? Might she have run blindly up to those charred ruins—

the place where she and John-Boy had first found each other?

"You got an idea?"

"No. I was just thinken. Maybe I'd just better start worken my way back toward home." If Jenny was on the mountain he wanted to be with her—alone, just the two of them.

"Okay. I'll go the other way. And if you find anythin' you let me know, John-Boy."

"I will."

John-Boy waited until the Sheriff drove off before he looked up at the mountain. He knew she was up there. She had to be there. Let her be there, he prayed as he headed out across the dark fields.

John-Boy stopped the minute he came within sight of the old house. In the darkness he could see only the black silhouette of the chimney rising from the ruins, and there was no movement in the shadows. For a minute fear stopped him from moving closer. If Jenny wasn't there he didn't know what he would do, or if he could bear it. To the anguish and despair that already gripped his heart would be added the painful knowledge that her flight had taken her away instead of closer to him.

And then he saw her. It was a small, almost invisible shadow crouched close to the chimney.

"Jenny!"

He was running, arms outstretched, almost to the house before the cry came from his throat. He half stumbled over the foundation, and then he was beside her, holding her, lifting her in his arms. "Jenny! Jenny, my love!"

He was crying, repeating her name, kissing her on the face and forehead, and then he held her tight, rocking her gently back and forth as he cried. And then his heart stopped beating.

John-Boy drew back, holding her at arm's length and stared into her face. She was looking back at him, but the face was expressionless, and her eyes seemed to be focused on something far beyond him.

"Jenny?"

She seemed not to hear. Her eyes drifted away, and she came limply forward as John-Boy drew her into his arms again. "Oh, my God," he breathed.

X

"Physically, there's not a thing wrong with Jenny," Dr. Shackleford said. "And there's no medicine I can prescribe that will do her much good. But I'll leave you some mild sedatives."

"Is she goin' to be all right?" John-Boy asked.

Dr. Shackleford sat on the edge of a straight-backed chair and stuffed his stethoscope into his black bag. He had been with Jenny for almost an hour before he came downstairs.

"That's hard to say, John-Boy. These things can be very complicated. Basically it's a case of shock. To a certain extent all of us shut out the rest of the world when we encounter extremely painful situations. It's a form of self-protection. We fear we can't cope with the problem, so we deny its existence. In most cases, however, we recover quickly. We take a deep breath, and one by one we accept the facts, knowing that time will eventually heal the wounds." He placed a small bottle on the table and snapped his bag shut.

"You think that'll happen with Jenny?"

Dr. Shackleford thought for a minute. "I hope so," he finally sighed. "But we have to appreciate the fact that Jenny has had more than her share of troubles. I understand she lost her mother not too long ago. No doubt that made her attachment to her father that much stronger. It's hard for us to imagine the emotional impact his death must be having on her. You say she hasn't spoken at all since you found her last night?"

"Not a word," John said. He and Olivia were sitting on the couch. The others were scattered around the room, with most of the children hovering by the kitchen door. Dr. Shackleford nodded.

"It could be a long process, I'm afraid."

The next question was hovering darkly in all of their minds. Mary Ellen asked it. "What if she never comes out of it?"

John-Boy almost wished it hadn't been asked. He looked quickly at Dr. Shackleford.

"There's that chance," he said. "If it goes on too long she will eventually lose touch with reality altogether."

John-Boy caught his breath. The thought of Jenny never speaking again, or spending the rest of her life in a mental institution, was inconceivable.

"But there certainly must be somethin' we can do," Olivia said.

Dr. Shackleford gave her a sympathetic smile. "I imagine you're already doing it. There's only one medicine I know of that can be any help at all. And you've got plenty of it right here."

"What's that, Doc?" John asked.

"It's all of you. Love. Jenny needs love and kindness more than anything. And I don't know where she can get more of it than right here." He picked up his bag and rose. "Well, I've got a long road ahead of me. I'll stop by again tomorrow if I get a chance."

John quickly got up and escorted him out the door. When they were gone Olivia smiled bravely. "Now, why don't you children all go outside for a while. We'll let you know if Jenny's any better."

Grandpa pulled himself to his feet. "Yeah. How's

that frog farm of yours comen along? Any of 'em ready to eat yet?"

"No, they're still tadpoles, Grandpa."

"Well, let's take a look. Maybe you're not feeden 'em right."

The children reluctantly followed Grandpa through the kitchen and out the back door.

"John-Boy, you'd better get some sleep. Why don't you go up in the boys' room and lie down? Grandma and I can sit with Jenny."

The words took a minute to penetrate John-Boy's dazed consciousness. She was right; he was exhausted. "Okay, Mama," he murmured. He got up and moved wearily toward the stairs.

He fell asleep the minute he dropped onto Jason's bed. Bringing Jenny down from the mountain, all his efforts to get her to speak, or cry, or even recognize his existence, and then the hours of sitting by her bed, talking to her, holding her hand, the long wait for the doctor, and then his disturbing statement that she might become a mental case; all these despairing frustrations suddenly numbed John-Boy into a deep and dreamless sleep.

Jenny was no better the next day. John-Boy, Grandma, and Olivia sat with her during the night, and after she nibbled at some breakfast they brought her down to a chair on the front porch. But Jenny still seemed lost somewhere behind her glazed, indifferent eyes. She might have been a hundred-year-old woman whose mind had receded into ancient memories.

They talked to her about her stepmother, telling her she would be home from the hospital the next morning. And when they were alone John-Boy held her hand and told her he loved her. But nothing seemed to penetrate. For long periods she stared vacantly toward the mountain, and then her eyes would close and her head droop as if in sleep.

John-Boy helped his father cut wood and the children did their chores or tended their tadpoles in subdued silence. The mood of the household was governed by Jenny's affliction, and when Dr. Shackleford came late in the afternoon, they all gathered silently on the porch while he talked to her.

Eula would be home in the morning, he said, and needed her very much. Then he talked about her father, and what a fine man he was, and how, more than anything, he wanted Jenny to have a rich and happy life. He spoke to her in a gentle voice, and pointed out that she was surrounded by very dear friends who loved her and needed her love in return.

For an instant, John-Boy thought Jenny was going to respond. While the doctor was talking, her eyes moved sharply to him and she seemed to be listening. But then they grew hazy and drifted away again.

Dr. Shackleford finally rose, and John-Boy and his father followed him to the car. "It's just going to take time," he repeated. "I talked to a friend of mine in Richmond this morning, and he said that in cases like this they've had some luck with electric shock treatments. But I'm not sure I'd recommend that just yet. Still, if it keeps up too much longer it would be wise to put her under the full-time care of specialists."

John-Boy shuddered at the words. They clearly meant an institution.

"Well, we'll keep tryen," John said.

Dr. Shackleford nodded grimly and closed the car door. "Yes, that's all any of us can do. I'll come by when I can."

John-Boy filled several pages of his notebook that night. For a while he sat beside Jenny, holding her hand, telling her of the house he would build when they got married, and how all of their children would look like her. And the children would raise tadpoles and sell frogs' legs, and they would have a dog named Not-So-Reckless. He rambled on and on, sometimes laughing at the things that came out of his mouth, altogether surprising himself that he could talk so long without a pause. But Jenny's distant silence finally brought him to a stop. Then he moved to his desk and got out his notebooks.

He was surprised to see how little he had written since the entry of the word *Jenny*. So much had happened since then. So many happy things, and so many sad things. John-Boy skipped several pages and wrote:

I fell in love with Jenny the moment she jumped up from that organ and ran out of the empty house. I didn't know I loved her then. That wonderful feeling was not to come until the next day. But right now, Jenny is lying on the bed next to me. Her eyes are closed and her arm is resting across her forehead. She is more beautiful than ever, and yet she is not here. Her thoughts are torn and twisted with grief and fear, and she has withdrawn into some darkly secure corner of her mind. She does not know I am here, nor that I am writing these things about her. In a few minutes I will leave her alone and go downstairs to sleep. She . . .

John-Boy couldn't go on. He took a deep breath and lifted his head for a minute in an effort to collect himself. And then Erin's voice came softly from the next room.

"Good night, John-Boy."

John-Boy looked over at the wall. "Good night, Erin."

"Good night, Jason."

"Good night, Erin."

The good-nights were soft and touched with sadness as they echoed through the house. John-Boy put his notebooks and pencil away and moved to the edge of the bed. "Good night, Jason," he called as he picked up Jenny's hand.

"Good night, John-Boy."

Jenny's eyes were open now, but they still had that vacant, faraway look.

"Good night, Elizabeth. Good night, Mary Ellen."

Elizabeth and Mary Ellen answered, and John-Boy responded to his mother's and Ben's voices.

Silence finally came. Bedsprings creaked in the next room, and then came his father's distant yawn. But John-Boy didn't move. He lifted a hand and touched Jenny's forehead, gently brushing back a stray hair. "Good night, Jenny," he murmured. He gazed at her for a minute, touching her cheek, and then his hand froze.

For an instant John-Boy distrusted his own senses. Through the past two days he had gazed into her eyes a thousand times, and each time he had seen nothing past the dull film of insensibility. But now the eyes were glistening. They were focused directly on him, and great wells of tears were beginning to tumble down her cheeks.

"Jenny!" he choked.

Her eyes closed tightly, her face contorted, and she was reaching for him, her body suddenly trembling with sobs. John-Boy drew her quickly into his arms. "It's all right, Jenny. It's just fine. Oh, dear Jenny, it's fine, it's fine."

"Hold me, John-Boy," she sobbed. "Please hold me."

He held her. He stroked her hair and kissed her on the forehead and on her damp cheeks and held her some more.

He didn't know whether to laugh or cry. He wanted to wake up the whole household with a shout of joy, at the same time he didn't want to move from her side ever again. He held her tightly, rocking her gently from side to side, and then he smiled as he looked over at the door.

His mother was there, blinking back the tears as she watched them.

XI

Dave Pendleton's funeral was held at the church the next day. In spite of his long absence from Walton's Mountain the mourners filled the pews and spilled out over the front steps. Dave Pendleton was greatly respected, and it was well known that except for his first wife's illness he would never have left the Mountain.

For John-Boy it was both a sad and a reassuring occasion. While the minister spoke of Dave Pendleton's warmth and love and humor, John-Boy couldn't help thinking of that night on the porch when they laughed so hard, and Dave Pendleton said there was nothing in the world that could make him any happier than he was then. John-Boy made no effort to stop the tears from running down his cheeks.

But seeing Jenny, and her efforts to console Eula through the service, brought him a renewed feeling of relief and joy.

She had left the house early that morning. She apologized for the troubles she had caused everybody, but everyone in the family had hugged and kissed her and told her how much they loved her. And then John-Boy's father had driven her home.

Dr. Shackleford permitted Eula to attend the funeral, but as quickly as it was over he drove her and Jenny back to their house. The others quietly dispersed, and Sheriff Bridges walked along with the Waltons.

"Too bad," he said, "Dave was a good man."

"You ever find out exactly what happened, Ep?" John asked.

It was just one of those things, the Sheriff told them. Dave and Eula were on a narrow dirt road, apparently taking the long way home, enjoying the ride, and a farmer came around a blind curve in his truck. The farmer didn't have a scratch on him. But he drove Dave and Eula to the hospital as quickly as he could.

"Say, John-Boy," Ep asked after a pause, "I don't s'pose you've been out to the Baldwins' in the last couple days, have you?"

"No," John-Boy told him.

"Well I'd sure like to know what's goen on out there. Been so busy I haven't had much time to keep a lookout for Cousin Homer. I don't s'pose you could run your truck out there and check for me, could you?"

John-Boy looked at his father, who glanced at Olivia.

"John-Boy doesn't have a driver's license, Sheriff. And I'm not too fond of his being around bootleggers anyway."

"Well, Miz Walton, John-Boy's a good enough driver. I've seen how he handles that truck of yours. And I don't reckon Cousin Homer's all that dangerous at all."

Olivia gave the Sheriff a dark look. She didn't approve of John-Boy driving without a license, and she approved even less of a sheriff who helped young men break the law. And her objections to John-Boy being around the Baldwins' had nothing to do with the possibility of Cousin Homer being dangerous.

"Let him go, Livvy." John smiled. "If he'll be helpen Ep round up a bootlegger I reckon we shouldn't stop him."

"Very well," Olivia sighed. "But I don't see why Ep

can't just go out there and arrest the whole bunch of 'em."

John-Boy was pleased with the decision. He could make his visit to the Baldwins' very short—just long enough to establish that Cousin Homer was still there—and then he could stop by the Pendletons' to see Jenny. When they all got home he changed quickly, wheeled the truck out to the road, and shoved the gas pedal to the floor.

The Baldwin sisters had heard about Dave Pendleton's death and Jenny's period of shock. As quickly as John-Boy turned off the motor they were hurrying across from the porch.

"My, it's just the saddest thing I ever heard, John-Boy."

"And poor little Jenny. I do hope she's mendin' satisfactorily. And Mrs. Pendleton. Just imagine, a new bride, and this terrible thing. I just sometimes wonder at the good Lord's way of managin' things."

One on each arm, they escorted John-Boy into the parlor where they insisted he sit down and tell them every detail of the last three days. They regretted very much that John-Boy hadn't brought Jenny with him so they could console the poor girl, and then they told him about their papa's funeral, and how people came from as far away as Baton Rouge to pay their respects.

John-Boy was preparing to ask about Homer Lee when he suddenly came into the room. His white suit was sparkling clean today, and he strode gravely across and took John-Boy's hand.

"My deepest sympathies, John-Boy. My dear cousins informed me of your loss, and of dear little Jeanie's distressful ordeal. A shame, a shame. The dear Lord works in mysterious ways, to be sure."

"Jenny," John-Boy corrected him.

"Of course. And a lovely thing she is. I trust that she has fully recovered, and poor Mrs. Pendleton is no longer sufferen?"

The Baldwin sisters smiled with admiration at their cousin's courtly manners. John-Boy nodded.

"I think they're both gonna be all right."

"Thank the good Lord for that."

Cousin Homer lowered himself into a chair and shook his head. "That such misfortune should befall us at a time when the Baldwin family is about to celebrate a joyous reunion is indeed an ill contrivance of fate. But as the poet said, 'Sorrow's crown of sorrow is rememberin' happier things.' "

"Now, isn't he just somethin'," Miss Emily said. "I declare, the way Cousin Homer can turn a phrase."

"Ah, bless you, dear Emily. And it is to happier things I think we should now address ourselves. Nature's greatest healer is good cheer. Don't you agree, John-Boy?"

"Yes sir."

For the first time John-Boy realized how bright and clean the house was. There were fresh cut flowers on every table, and all the old family pictures he'd brought down from the attic were now dusted and polished and hanging on the walls. With sudden alarm he also realized that this was Saturday, the day of the reunion— and the day he was supposed to deliver the battery to Cousin Homer. But Cousin Homer appeared to be perfectly at ease, and the ladies were now consulting their guest list, apparently resuming their excited speculations from before his arrival.

"I just can't imagine where we're goen to put all these people if they're expectin' to stay overnight," Miss Mamie said. "But then I remember Third Cousin Efram always seemed to enjoy sleepen in his car. He's such a hardy soul."

"Yes," Miss Emily agreed, "and I do hope Cousin Cora comes. Remember how sweet she was to come and stay when Papa died?"

Cousin Homer smiled wistfully. "Ah, yes, dear Cousin Cora. Such charmen feet. A lovely lady."

"Oh, Cousin Cora's sure to come. Washington, D.C., isn't all that far away. Cousin Tyrone is the one I'm dyin' to see."

Miss Emily gave her a surprised look. "I thought Cousin Tyrone was the one they had to . . . confine."

"Oh, he's perfectly harmless, Emily. It was those

nosy neighbors who were so suspicious because he built that chariot and drove it around the place."

"I would have loved to have ridden in a chariot! Wouldn't you, John-Boy?"

John-Boy smiled. "Yes'm."

"Well, don't you two give up hope," Miss Mamie said. "Perhaps Cousin Tyrone will drive his chariot over from Buckin'ham County."

Miss Emily sighed happily. "Oh, it's goen to be such a grand party. I declare, I just can't hardly wait for the first ones to start arriven."

John-Boy glanced at the big grandfather clock, but its hands were still frozen at twelve minutes after two. He guessed it was a little past noon by now. He cleared his throat and moved forward on the chair. "Is there anythen you ladies will be wanten me for? If not, I expect I ought to be getten home."

"Oh dear, now I just don't know," Miss Mamie said, looking around. "I do think just about everythen's been done. But we'd certainly love to have you at the reunion, John-Boy."

Cousin Homer seemed to come quickly alert. "Ah, now, Miss Mamie, I do think everythen is about as nearly perfect as it could be. Your charmin' abode could be no more refreshin' and spotlessly hospitable than its present condition, and I can imagine no more gracious hostesses than you two lovely ladies. However, there is one small item, one very last touch of elegance, that I fear we have neglected."

"Neglected? Is somethen wrong, Cousin Homer?"

"Wrong? Ah, ladies, to suggest somethin' is amiss is an audacity far beyond consideration. It is a small thing, perhaps, but it comes to mind only with fond reflections upon the memory of your dear, departed father."

"On Papa? I declare, Cousin Homer, I just can't fathom what you're talken about."

"Branch water, Miss Emily."

"Branch water?"

"Branch water!" Miss Mamie exclaimed. "Why Cousin Homer is perfectly right, sister. Papa always took his Recipe with branch. And a good many of the Baldwins still do!"

"That's right! I do recall now! How clever of you to have remembered, Cousin Homer."

"To have forgotten would be the gravest expression of ingratitude, dear Emily. And as I recall, it was a very special branch water, taken from a very special place."

"Yes. Don't you remember, Mamie? It was about a mile up the stream, wasn't it?"

"My!" Miss Mamie sighed. "Do you suppose it's still there? Papa's old cup still hangen from that dogwood tree?"

"We could certainly look. Cousin Homer and John-Boy could go up the stream. I'm sure they can find it."

"What pleasure it would give me," Cousin Homer said, "to find the very cup with which Judge Morley Baldwin so lovin'ly dipped the sparklin' nectar from that bubblin' brook. Alas, however, it is a pleasure I must forsake until a more propitious time. My leg, I'm afraid, prohibits contemplatin' what, under other circumstances, would be a most delightful outin'."

"Your leg? Have you injured yourself, Cousin Homer?"

"I'll bet you did it while you were pushen the car," Miss Emily said. "Cousin Homer thought he could get our car started if he could push it out to the road. But the old thing was just too heavy for him."

Cousin Homer lifted a protesting hand. "A matter of minor consequence, my dear. A small sprain. But I am certain John-Boy will have no difficulty locatin' the place in question."

They all smiled at John-Boy. "Of course not," Miss Emily said. "You wouldn't mind doin' that, would you, John-Boy?"

"I'm afraid I've never been up that stream before, Miss Emily."

"Oh, you won't have any problem. It's a lovely little place in a grove of spruce trees. And you just can't miss that charmin' little dogwood at the bend in the stream. The cup is hangin' right out over the water."

Miss Mamie was already on her feet heading for the kitchen. "I'll get you a container, John-Boy."

"It's goen to be so lovely havin' branch water," Miss Emily said. "Cousin Homer, I think that's just the cleverest thing! I declare, it's goen to make our party just like old times again!"

The container John-Boy carried into the woods was a ten-gallon cask with a wooden bung. He also had instructions from Miss Mamie to rinse it out thoroughly before filling it. The directions for finding the particular spot they had in mind were a little vague. Miss Mamie thought it was about a half mile upstream; Miss Emily thought it was closer to a mile, and Cousin Homer was sure it was much more than that. John-Boy suspected there wasn't a whole lot of difference between the water downstream, and that running under the dogwood tree with the hanging cup. But it seemed to mean a lot to the Baldwin sisters.

What puzzled him was Cousin Homer. When John-Boy left the house Homer limped along a few yards to get him started in the right direction, and John-Boy told him he would drive into Ike Godsey's and get the new battery as soon as he got back with the water.

"Don't worry about it, John-Boy." Cousin Homer smiled. "Plenty of time to take care of that. And with all the relatives comin' this afternoon, I don't expect I'll have a chance to get away anyhow." Then he clapped John-Boy on the back and grinned after him until he was out of sight.

Cousin Homer's enthusiasm for the reunion party didn't make any sense. At least it didn't go along with the way Sheriff Bridges had it figured out. If Homer didn't get the Recipe out of the Baldwin house before all those relatives came there wasn't likely to be any left for him to sell. And people would probably be arriving within four or five hours.

It was possible, John-Boy guessed, that Cousin Homer had given up the whole idea. Maybe the kindness and love of the Baldwin sisters had inspired him to walk a narrower path from now on. It was not likely, but such things sometimes happened.

John-Boy walked for twenty minutes before he found the hanging cup. There were times when the spruce groves were so thick he had to make long detours around them to follow the stream, and other times he had to tramp through boggy meadows. Then he was suddenly there, at a heavily shaded bend where the dark water made soft sucking sounds as it flowed under the moss-covered bank. John-Boy was surprised; the water did look different. And the old blue-enameled cup was hanging from a piece of twisted wire, dangling only a few inches above the water's surface.

The water was amazingly cool and refreshing. John-Boy took a long drink and stretched out on the shady grass for a few minutes before he filled the cask. It was a beautiful spot. He wished Jenny had been able to come along with him. But he would have plenty of time to bring her up here. As soon as her stepmother was fully recovered they would have the rest of spring and all summer to explore the brooks and streams for miles around. John-Boy smiled and closed his eyes for a minute. Thank you, Lord, he thought, for bringing Jenny back. And take care of Dave Pendleton. You'll like him very much.

John-Boy didn't notice it at first. Lugging the ten-gallon cask down the stream was a harder job than he had anticipated, and when he got to the house his arms and shoulders were aching, and his only thought was to get the thing inside and catch his breath. But there was something odd about the Baldwin house—something not in its right place. And then he stopped, staring.

The truck was gone. He had parked it under the big tree over the garage—he was certain of that. But now there was no sign of it; no vehicles of any kind in sight. John-Boy's heart pounded wildly as he headed for the back door.

"Oh, there you are, John-Boy." Miss Mamie smiled in the kitchen. "Did you find the branch water?"

"Yes'm, I did. But Miss Mamie, my daddy's truck is gone."

The news had no visible effect on Miss Mamie.

"Yes, Cousin Homer just borrowed it for a little while. Let's put the water here on the sink, John-Boy. That'll be fine."

John-Boy put the cask down and felt in his pocket. "But I still have the keys, Miss Mamie. How——?"

"Yes. Cousin Homer said it wouldn't hurt the truck any. He just did somethen with those little wires, and it started just fine. Cousin Homer is awfully clever."

"But, Miss Mamie——"

"Now don't you worry about a thing, John-Boy. Cousin Homer will only be gone for a little while. And he's goen to replenish any gas he uses."

"Did he say where he was goen?"

Miss Mamie brightened. "Oh, you know how thoughtful Cousin Homer is. He decided to check the train station over in town to see if any of the Baldwins have shown up yet."

In town? That meant Charlottesville, and it probably meant Daisy Burgess's beauty shop. "Miss Mamie, you know all those jars of Recipe you been maken?"

"Yes. We've got almost three hundred of them, John-Boy. I declare, I think those shelves are just about to burst with all those jars."

"Miss Mamie, I think we ought to take a look at those shelves."

"Oh, I'm sure they won't really break. Papa built them himself, and I expect they'll just last forever."

"Can we look at them, Miss Mamie?"

Miss Mamie gave him an indulgent smile and headed for the Recipe room. "I declare, John-Boy, you're just the most conscientious young man. Just like your father and your granddaddy. It's just a pleasure to——"

Miss Mamie stopped abruptly in the center of the Recipe room, her smile suddenly turning to dismay. "Oh, my!" she breathed. "Oh, dear me! Emily!" she cried.

John-Boy was fairly certain the shelves would be empty, but still his heart sank. The jars were gone and Cousin Homer was gone, and Sheriff Bridges was probably nowhere to be found.

John-Boy had never used a telephone before. Ike Godsey showed him how to crank the handle, and then the voice of Fanny Tatum came mysteriously through the black piece John-Boy held at his ear.

"Hullo?" he said as Ike had instructed him.

"Hello? That you, John-Boy? John-Boy Walton? You got a telephone out at your place now?"

"No, Miss Fanny, I'm talken from Ike Godsey's."

"Well, you say 'Hey' to Ike for me. How's your mama, John-Boy?"

John-Boy wasn't sure if all this was required for him to get a message to Sheriff Bridges. Altogether it was a strange sensation to be talking into a perforated black hole and be hearing Fanny Tatum's voice at his ear. He looked apprehensively at the mechanism and glanced over at Ike. "Miss Fanny says to tell you 'Hey,' Ike. And Mama's just fine, Miss Fanny."

"Tell Fanny I appreciate it," Ike said.

"Ike says he appreciates it, Miss Fanny."

"Well, he's sure welcome, John-Boy. Wasn't that a nice funeral this mornen? I declare I don't think I ever saw so many pretty flowers."

"Yes'm. Miss Fanny, is there some kind of way I can use this thing to talk to Sheriff Bridges?"

"You sure can, John-Boy, if he's home. You just hold on a minute."

Ep Bridges answered sleepily, but came wide awake when John-Boy told him what happened at the Baldwins'.

"Three hundred jars? And he took it all in your daddy's truck?"

"Yes sir, and I'd say that was about an hour and a half ago, so I reckon he's already been to Charlottesville by now."

"Lordy me," Ep groaned. "Well, you better get off the phone, John-Boy, so I can make some calls. That scalawag's likely roarin' through Carolina by now."

"You want me to call Daisy Burgess's beauty shop?" Fanny Tatum broke in.

"No," Ep said, "I wanta talk to the state police in Richmond."

"But Ep, if you call Daisy's you can find out if Cousin Homer's been there yet."

"Damn it, Fanny, will you just take care of the telephones and let me handle the police work?"

"Well it seems to me that . . ."

John-Boy took the receiver from his ear and looked questioningly at Ike.

"Just put it in that little hook, John-Boy. Then you give the crank a turn or two to let Fanny know you're done."

John-Boy did what Ike told him, then looked at the silent mechanism. Sheriff Bridges's house was more than a mile away—it just didn't seem possible that he had been talking directly to him.

"What's your daddy gonna say 'bout his truck turnen up missen?" Ike asked.

In his concern to report to the Sheriff, John-Boy hadn't thought much about that. But his father sure wasn't going to be happy about it. "I don't know. But I expect I'll find out soon enough." He dug some money from his pocket. "Here's four more dollars for the washen machine, Ike."

Ike smiled and took the money.

"That makes ten dollars total," John-Boy said.

Ike gave him a quick glance and scratched his chin for a minute. "Yes," he said hesitantly, "I guess that's about right."

"That's exactly right, Ike. Ten more dollars and it's paid for."

Ike still appeared uncertain. "Well, don't you worry none about it, John-Boy," he said and made out a receipt. "And I'll hang a Sold sign on it so's nobody else can have it."

"But I only owe ten dollars more. That's right, ain't it, Ike?"

"Like I said, John-Boy, don't worry about it. The price of the washer was twenty dollars, and you got receipts sayin' you paid ten. That's clear enough."

John-Boy looked at the receipt and glanced uneasily at Ike. It seemed clear enough all right, but he had the feeling Ike was up to something. But Ike wouldn't try to cheat him, would he? Or would he?

The bell tinkled on the door and Ike turned away with a broad smile. "Afternoon, Miz Merrill."

"And then when I got back," John-Boy said to his father, "the truck was gone, and Miss Mamie said he'd gone over to town to pick up people for the reunion. And all the Recipe jars were gone. I guess he did somethen with the ignition wires to make it run, because I was careful to take the key, Daddy." John-Boy handed over the key to prove he had taken the proper precautions.

John Walton was surprised by the announcement, but he had a hard time holding back a smile when he pictured Cousin Homer Lee bouncing down the road with close to three hundred jars of Recipe in the back of that old truck. He and Grandpa were sawing wood when John-Boy came trudging up the road with his tail between his legs. John glanced at Grandpa, who was smiling openly.

"You say he took all the Recipe?"

"Every last drop. And Daddy, they got a hundred and twenty-seven people comen to the house this afternoon."

That was even funnier. Picturing a hundred and twenty-seven Baldwins in one place, and not a drop of Recipe—that was like a whole herd of thirsty cattle finding their water hole dry. The roar and moaning of Baldwins was likely to be heard through the whole valley before sundown.

John-Boy saw his father glance at Grandpa, and then the two of them suddenly burst out laughing. His father stopped after a minute, but then couldn't control himself and started all over again.

"There's not a drop of Recipe in the whole place?" he asked incredulously when he caught his breath.

"No sir."

Grandpa guffawed again, and sat down on a log, slapping his knee. "Oh, what I wouldn't give to see that!" he choked. "A hundred and twenty-seven of 'em!" and laughed harder yet.

John-Boy stared from one to the other, wondering

for a minute if they understood about the truck being stolen.

"John-Boy," his father finally said, "that's about the funniest thing I've heard in years. I expect that's goen to be the most memorable reunion in the history of Walton's Mountain."

"But Daddy, how are you gonna get along without your truck? What're you gonna do?"

John thought a minute and smiled. "What I'm gonna do, son, is just keep right on cuttin' wood. That ol' truck is such a broken-down eyesore, Cousin Homer'll be picked up in no time atall. I wouldn't be a bit surprised if he don't bring it back himself and hand it over in disgust."

John-Boy doubted that. But his father's words relieved him some.

"You goen to stay here and help us?" Grandpa asked.

There were a half-dozen heavy logs waiting to be rough cut, and Grandpa looked like he'd welcome a rest. "I'd sure like to, Grandpa. But I promised the ladies I'd come back and help with the reunion."

His father laughed again. "They're sure enough goen to need all the help they can get when all them Baldwins show up with their tongues hangin' out. You might be smart to take along my rifle, John-Boy."

Grandpa grinned, and the laughter started again as John-Boy headed for the house.

John-Boy decided not to mention the disappearance of the truck to his mother. She would not take such a casual attitude as his father, nor was she likely to let him return to the Baldwins'. But John-Boy had no need to worry. His mother was involved in other, more distracting problems.

The kitchen looked as if a tornado had struck it—or more accurately as if a tornado had hit the Richmond library and carried all the reading material over the mountains and deposited it in the Waltons' kitchen.

Four years ago John-Boy's father had helped a family named Beckwith when they were moving away from Walton's Mountain. Among the many things George Beckwith decided to throw away rather than take with him was a complete set of *National Geographic* magazines dating back to 1912. To Olivia's consternation, instead of taking them to the dump, John had brought them all home, and since that time they had occupied a dark and forbidden corner of the cellar. Olivia had no objection to the scientific and cultural knowledge presented in the magazines, and on occasions they were very helpful to the children's homework. But what she couldn't understand was why it was necessary for the editors to print full-color pictures of unclothed aborigines, men and women. Whether people were dark-skinned or not, they were still human beings, and the laws of civilized, God-fearing decency still applied. When the children needed information about odd places such as Nicaragua or Nepal, Olivia went to the cellar herself to scan the indexed back covers for the appropriate issues. Only then, after the magazine was carefully scrutinized and the objectionable photographs torn from its pages, was the copy brought upstairs for consultation. But today, Mary Ellen, Ben, Jim-Bob, and Elizabeth had carted the entire library up to the kitchen before Olivia realized what was going on.

"It is not necessary to look through all the pages," she was telling them when John-Boy came in. "Just read the contents on the front cover and it tells you exactly what's in each magazine."

Her words were having no effect. Elizabeth was staring wide-eyed at pictures of seals, Ben was engrossed in an article about mountain climbing, and Mary Ellen and Jim-Bob were methodically going through every page of every magazine.

"What's goen on?" John-Boy asked.

"Frogs," Mary Ellen said.

Erin, who was wiping dishes and seemed to be enjoying the spectacle, smiled airily. "Mary Ellen's tadpoles all ran away.'

"They didn't run away," Mary Ellen muttered. "Frogs don't run, they hop."

"Well, however they did it, the tadpoles all turned into frogs and disappeared."

John-Boy still didn't understand why the place was cluttered with magazines. He got some liver sausage from the refrigerator to make a sandwich. "Isn't that what you wanted? I mean didn't you expect 'em to turn into frogs?"

"But not *that* kind of frogs," Erin said smugly.

"What kind of frogs?"

Olivia decided to put an end to Erin's contentious comments before Mary Ellen exploded. "The frog farm didn't turn out very well, John-Boy. The tadpoles all turned into frogs and hopped away this mornen."

"They all climbed trees." Erin smiled. "They were *tree* frogs."

"Oh."

Mary Ellen and Jim-Bob were turning pages at a furious pace now, controlling their anger.

"It seems to me," Erin said, "a person ought to find out the difference between tree frogs and bullfrogs *first, before* he starts collectin' tadpoles."

That was the final straw for Mary Ellen. She slammed her magazine down and grabbed up another one. "You're the kind of person who always waits until someone falls down and breaks his leg, and *then* you say, 'Watch your step.' But the only thing you know how to do is brush your hair!"

"All right, children," Olivia said. "That's enough. Now clear a place for John-Boy so he can eat at the table."

"Mary Ellen," Ben suddenly said, "maybe we oughta raise ladybugs. It says here they use them in California to protect the crops from aphids. What's an aphid?"

"We're goen to raise frogs' legs," Mary Ellen said emphatically. "Just forget about ladybugs and find somethin' about bullfrog tadpoles."

"Somebody tore a page out of this issue," Jim-Bob said. "Look at this, right in the middle of a story about pygmies. Why would someone do that?"

"Never mind," Olivia said quickly and took the magazine. "Now let's just get this organized and do things sensibly. Why don't you all let *me* read the contents on the covers, and then if there's anything about frogs or tadpoles we'll all read it carefully."

XII

John-Boy was a little surprised when he came in sight of the Baldwin house again. It was after four o'clock and he expected at least two or three cars to be parked in front. But there was not a vehicle—not even a chariot—in sight. Nor were the Baldwin sisters on the porch, or anywhere to be seen. John-Boy had to knock several times before Miss Mamie answered.

She let him in with a desperately anxious look. "You didn't happen to see any Baldwins lost on the highway, did you, John-Boy? Anyone asken to find their way here?"

"No ma'am."

Miss Mamie led him into the parlor where Miss Emily was sitting on one of the love seats in her frilly gown.

"I'm afraid it's only John-Boy," she said, and Miss Emily sagged with disappointment.

"Oh, dear, I'm afraid nobody at all is comen, sister. I

was just sure Ashley Longworth would have arrived by this time. Do sit down, John-Boy."

"We're just goen to have to face the facts, Emily. It's been twenty-five years since you've seen Ashley Longworth."

John-Boy had never seen Miss Emily looking so pretty. With the skirt of her dress hooped out in a beautiful semicircle and her hair in a mass of dangling curls, she looked like a picture somebody had painted. But she looked as if she were about to cry as she gazed at a scattering of opened envelopes on the table. They all seemed covered with red and black ink from rubber stamps.

"Still, it's not like Ashley not to favor us with a reply," she said.

Miss Mamie picked up one of the envelopes. "He couldn't favor us with a reply, Emily, because he never received the letter. It says, 'Return to Sender—Address Unknown.' I'm sure he would have replied if he had received it."

Miss Emily seemed only mildly reassured. "Imagine that splendid young man haven no address. I would think you could just address it, 'Ashley Longworth, The World,' and it would eventually get to him."

From the number of envelopes on the table, John-Boy guessed about half of them had been returned for lack of a correct address. The other invitations must have been lost in the mail, or the people hadn't bothered to answer. On one of them John-Boy could see the word "Deceased," in red ink. But it was apparent that the Baldwin sisters' reunion was not going to take place.

"Your dress looks real pretty, Miss Emily," John-Boy offered. "I expect you two ladies are just about the prettiest in all Virginia."

The compliment seemed to catch them both by surprise. Miss Mamie blushed, while Miss Emily smiled brightly. "Why, John-Boy, what a nice thing to say. I declare, Mamie, these Walton men just never fail to be as nice as all get-out. I've always said you can count on a Walton."

But the weight of the returned invitations was too

much to escape. Miss Emily looked at them with a sigh, then rose and moved slowly to the window.

"I had so looked forward to singen 'round the piano," she said. She lifted the frail curtain from the window and peered up the road as far as she could. "And the sound of children's voices. You know, John-Boy, there were goen to be thirty-seven children here today. Can't you just imagine all those happy voices?"

Miss Mamie smiled softly at the thought. "I expect there's no reason for you to be stayen here, John-Boy. I'm sure you'll be wanten to see your Jenny sometime today."

"Yes'm," John-Boy said. But he felt terrible leaving the two ladies alone. All the pictures of relatives hanging on the walls seemed to make things even worse. And the desertion of Cousin Homer, their guest of honor, must have been the cruelest blow of all. "I don't really have to go. I could stay and talk if you want."

Miss Emily came back from the window. "Now you just don't be silly, John-Boy Walton. Mamie and I will just have ourselves a nice supper and go to bed. And I just know Miss Jenny is achin' for you to come around and see her and her poor mother."

"Emily is right. You just run along now, John-Boy. Just 'cause our guests couldn't come is no reason why Jenny Pendleton's favorite guest can't come a-callin'. And you be sure to give them all our love."

John-Boy promised to do that. But walking home he couldn't help thinking about how heartbroken the two sisters must have been when those letters all came back. And then their brave attempts to appear lighthearted as they forced him out the door seemed about the saddest thing of all.

He guessed they would spend the rest of the evening taking down all those pictures. And then Miss Emily would put away her dress and never take it out of the trunk again.

"I declare, Mamie, these Walton men just never fail to be as nice as all get-out. I've always said you can count on a Walton." Remembering the words, and the brief, happy look on Miss Emily's face when she said them, brought an extra sadness to John-Boy. He guessed that tonight more than ever before in their lives the Baldwin sisters needed someone to count on. But from the looks of things it didn't appear like a single person was going to show up to help them.

John-Boy had a pleasant surprise when he arrived home. He had intended to clean up as quickly as possible and go directly over to Jenny's house. But when he opened the door to the kitchen he faced a crowd of laughing, talking people, with Jenny Pendleton the center of attention.

"Look who's here, John-Boy," his father called out. "Jenny Pendleton, and she's maken up for them two days she wouldn't talk to any of us."

Jenny was standing by the sink, and she quickly came across and took John-Boy's hand.

"We don't want no kissen here in the kitchen," Grandpa said. "We don't want you two embarrassin' Grandma now." He laughed and slapped his knee.

John-Boy felt his face flush, but he put an arm around Jenny and smiled. "Okay, Grandpa."

"It won't embarrass me," his father said, and everyone looked expectantly at John-Boy. He gave Jenny a quick kiss on the forehead.

"You call that a kiss?" Grandpa shouted. "Why, a thing like that makes me 'shamed to be a Walton. John, that boy ain't your son, is he? He shore ain't my grandson."

They all laughed and John-Boy squeezed Jenny closer to his side. "How's Eula?"

Jenny was as relieved as John-Boy to have the subject changed. "She's much better, and Mrs. Shackleford came over to stay with her for a while."

"Get yourself cleaned up, John-Boy," Olivia smiled. "We're all eatin' in about two minues."

"Yeah," Grandpa said. "And take that girl somewhere so you can do some real kissen."

Grandma said grace, giving thanks for Jenny's and Eula's recovery, and asked the Lord to take care of Dave Pendleton. As quickly as she finished John Walton grinned and started the food circulating. "Well, John-Boy, how's the big reunion goen out at the Baldwins'? Them relatives shooten at each other yet?"

"There ain't no reunion, Daddy. Nobody showed up."

Everyone looked up in surprise. "They must of heard about Cousin Homer runnen off with the Recipe." Grandpa laughed.

"Not one person came?" Jenny asked with concern.

John-Boy told them about all the invitations coming back, and how the two ladies had gotten themselves all dressed up.

"Too bad," his father said. "But haven no Recipe around, maybe they're lucky nobody came."

John-Boy glanced cautiously at his mother. "Any news about the truck, Daddy?"

"Not yet. But I expect it'll be back here by mornen."

There was no comment from his mother, and John-Boy guessed she'd been told what happened.

"Ike says Ep Bridges was madder'n a wet goose." Grandpa laughed. "Filled up his gas tank and headed off to Charlottesville like a bat out of . . ."

Grandma gave him a sharp kick. "You hush, old man!"

Grandpa winced from the pain. "I was goen to say, like a witch on a broom. What's the matter with that?"

"When did you see Ike Godsey?" John asked. It was an indifferent question, but it seemed to unnerve Grandpa for a minute. He glanced around and shrugged. "We was just chewen the fat. I took a walk over there this afternoon."

John-Boy's father laughed. "You figure maybe Cousin Homer sold some of that Recipe to Ike, Grandpa?"

"You better not bring none of that Recipe in this house," Grandma said.

"No such thing, old woman. When a man reaches ninety-five he's entitled to sit around the cracker barrel on occasion."

"Hmmph! Yesterday you were ninety-eight, and last week you were ninety-two."

"That's right. And them two numbers averages out

to ninety-five, which is correct, more or less." Grandpa grinned around the table, then stretched his arms from his cuffs preparing to cut his corn kernels off the cob.

There was finally silence at the table and John-Boy put his fork down on the plate. "Mama ... and everybody ... I'm goen to ask you all somethin'. And I expect maybe you're goen to think I'm crazy."

Olivia smiled. "Ask anyway, John-Boy."

"Well, like I told you, I think the Baldwin sisters are right broken up over no one comen. I mean, they're pretenden like it's not important, but I could kind of tell they're feelen pretty bad."

His mother frowned suspiciously at him, as if anticipating what he was going to say.

"What were you goen to ask us, son?"

John-Boy took a deep breath. "Couldn't we all just put on some nice clothes and go over there, and spend the evenin' with 'em. They're sitten there all alone in that big empty house. And they just love children."

His mother gaped at him as if he had suggested they make a social call on the devil. She glanced at John and back to John-Boy. "John-Boy, I think it's enough that you've been spenden so much time out there. I have no desire for any of the younger children to be within five miles of that Recipe of theirs."

"Amen," Grandma agreed.

"But Mama, there's not a thing in the house stronger'n lemonade now. Cousin Homer took all the Recipe away."

"That's true, Livvy," John said.

Grandpa was suddenly eating at full speed. "I don't know about the rest of you, but I'm goen."

"Then so am I," Grandma announced. "To keep an eye on you, old man."

John-Boy felt Jenny's hand touch his, then squeeze it under the table. She was watching his mother, who appeared to be reconsidering.

"Well, I can't say that I approve of the things Miss Emily and Miss Mamie do. But ... well ..." She smiled thoughtfully. "It does break my heart to think of those poor old things sufferen like that."

"Can we all go, Mama?"

She looked across the table. "You think that green dress of mine would be all right, John?"

"Livvy, in that green dress you look like a princess. I just hope a princess won't mind goen to the grand ball with a country woodcutter. Come on, everybody, let's get a move on!"

If Olivia had reservations they were quickly dispelled. As soon as they were all dressed and headed up the road Grandpa moved to the front of the group and lifted his arm. "Onward Christian s-o-o-o-l-diers . . ." he boomed out in solemn tones, and they all joined in.

This was followed by "Rock of Ages" and then "The Battle Hymn of the Republic," each in stirringly louder tones than the other. Whether Grandpa deliberately paced them or not was hard to say, but when they came into sight of the Baldwins' house they were in the midst of a rousing chorus of "Dixie."

John-Boy tried to imagine what was going on inside the Baldwin sisters' house. When the Walton family was within a hundred feet of the front porch he saw a curtain pulled discreetly to the side. Within a couple seconds the other side was parted, and then he could make out the two startled faces.

The Waltons spread out in front of the porch to finish the song. Grandpa mounted the steps, both arms now directing with great sweeps, and they all boomed out the final line, "Awaaaaaaay down south in Dixxxxxxxiiiieeeee!"

The curtains dropped back into place and a second later the front door swung open. Miss Emily and Miss Mamie were speechless. Normally they were all smiles and ready to gush and swoon with greetings for callers. But this evening neither of them seemed able to speak. They were blinking, their mouths moving, and tears were standing in their eyes, but not a sound came out.

"Happy reunion, ladies!" Grandpa roared, and then the others repeated it as they crowded forward.

"Well, I declare," Miss Emily finally managed. "Well, I declare!"

"Evenen, Miss Emily," John-Boy grinned. "Evenen, Miss Mamie."

"Well, I declare! I do declare, John-Boy, how nice of you all to come a-callin'."

"Miz Walton, what a pleasure this is! It is *indeed* a pleasure to have you all in our home! Come in! Ever'body come in! And you brought all of your lovely children! Oh, my, Emily! Oh, dear me!"

It took several minutes for everyone to get inside and for Miss Mamie and Miss Emily to examine each of the children and rave about how big and handsome they had all grown. And then they got all fluttery again and escorted Olivia and Grandma to honored positions in the love seats.

John-Boy had never seen two people quite so beside themselves with happiness. They cooed over the children, kept repeating what a pleasure and joy it was to have so many callers, and then they rushed to the kitchen and began carting out an incredible array of cakes and pies and sweets. And with every compliment Miss Emily's eyes would fill with happy tears and she would rush out to the kitchen and bring more.

"Cousin Homer took every drop of the Recipe, eh?" Grandpa asked when they all finally settled down with coffee and lemonade.

"Every single drop, Mr. Walton." Miss Emily laughed. "And I just hate to think how disappointed all the Baldwins might have been if they'd come. I declare, maybe it's a blessen disguised by the Lord."

"Hallelujah!" Grandma smiled.

"He just cleared those shelves clean as can be," Miss Mamie said. "Would you all like to see?"

Grandpa quickly put his cake aside. "Sure would, Miss Mamie."

Olivia suggested that it wasn't necessary for everyone to go look at the Recipe room, but her words were lost in the clatter of plates and eagerly rising children. Miss Emily and Miss Mamie led the way, and Olivia and Grandma reluctantly brought up the rear.

The shelves were indeed all empty. But as an academic exercise—in the interests of discerning just how thorough Cousin Homer had been—Grandpa and John searched all the dark corners, peered into empty milk cans, checked the closet, and felt deep into the crevices of the two overstuffed chairs.

"Yes sirree," Grandpa finally sighed, "You've got to hand it to Cousin Homer. He sure didn't miss a drop."

" 'Pears that way," Grandma said dryly from the door.

"I must say," Miss Mamie smiled, "on those occasions when Cousin Homer took it into his mind to do somethen, he always did a fine job of it."

"Well, Grandpa," John grinned, "shall we go have some more lemonade?"

"I do believe that would hit the spot, John. You ladies do make fine lemonade."

After more lemonade was served, the party took a turn more to Olivia and Grandma's liking. Grandma played the piano, and for an hour and a half they all sang songs. Grandpa danced his Irish jig again, and John-Boy attempted a Virginia reel with Jenny, to the accompaniment of great laughter and advice from the Baldwin sisters.

The party was a great success, and by ten o'clock everyone was stuffed with goodies and exhausted, and they all bid the happy ladies good night.

There was one more surprise for everybody that night. When the Waltons arrived home, the old truck was parked back by the barn and Ike Godsey was waiting for them on the front porch.

"Yep, they caught ol' Cousin Homer down by Danville." He laughed. "Guess he was maken for Greensboro, and he still had a hundred jars of Recipe left."

"You mean that old truck got all the way to the state border?" John asked, and they all looked at the dusty truck with admiration.

"Sure enough did. Cousin Homer left a trail of Recipe jars clear across the countryside. That's how Ep followed him. Found Cousin Homer sellen the stuff right off the back of the truck at the Danville County Fair. Homer claimed it was genuine, certified, bonded patent medicine guaranteed to cure rheumatism, corns, and fallen hair. He was also winken at the crowd and tellen 'em it contained only sixty percent alcohol. Ep Bridges arrested him himself and confiscated all the Recipe that was left. For evidence, of course."

Ike grinned and followed the family into the house. "So Ep had some young fella drive yer truck back, John, and then I drove her out here for you. She's in fine shape."

"I sure do appreciate that, Ike."

"All right, children," Olivia said, "time for everybody to be in bed."

"Uh, Miz Walton," Ike suddenly said, "could the kids stay up a little bit longer. Just a few minutes?"

It was an odd request that brought an immediate silence from the family.

"What do you mean, Ike?" Olivia asked, "I don't understand."

Ike smiled again. "You'll understand in a minute, Miz Walton. If everybody'll just come in the kitchen." Ike glanced slyly at Grandpa and gave his head a toss.

Grandpa seemed to understand the gesture and took John-Boy's arm. "Come on, John-Boy." He smiled. "You gotta help me a minute out here."

"What in the world's goen on?" Olivia protested.

"You just wait in the kitchen," Grandpa said, and took John-Boy out the back door.

"Grandpa, what—?" John-Boy caught his breath as the door banged behind them. There, standing by the back steps, was the secondhand washing machine he'd been buying from Ike. An old blanket half covered it, but there was no question about what it was. And now it was cleaned up and as shiny as a new one. "What's goen on, Grandpa?"

"All paid for, John-Boy. Your ten dollars and my ten dollars makes twenty."

"You paid Ike ten dollars too?"

Grandpa shrugged. "Well, it was my fault the whole thing came up in the first place. And I earned a little money out at the Baldwins' while you was taken care of Jenny. Now you just get ahold of that side over there."

Ike held the door open. Grandpa made sure the blanket was pulled down far enough to disguise the whole thing, and they edged their way through the door and set the thing in front of the refrigerator.

"What on earth?" Olivia exclaimed. "What are you two doen?"

"You do it, John-Boy," Grandpa said and stepped aside. "Unveil her!"

John-Boy smiled at Jenny and then over at his mother. Only his father, Grandpa, Jenny, and Ike Godsey knew what was under the blanket. The others all wore puzzled looks. John-Boy grasped the middle of the blanket and swept it off.

There was a gasp of surprise and pleasure from everyone but Olivia. She looked as if she had been struck dumb. Her mouth dropped open and she stared at the machine, but no words came out.

"Oh, Mama, it's beautiful!" Erin cried.

"A washen machine!" Elizabeth squealed and ran forward to touch it.

The others were all grinning, looking at Olivia, but she still seemed paralyzed.

"What's the matter, Mama," Mary Ellen said. "It's a real washen machine."

"None of it came out of the house money, Livvy," John said. "John-Boy and Grandpa earned every cent of it themselves." He sat down and put an arm around her, grinning.

But still Olivia was speechless. Tears suddenly filled her eyes and she shook her head, trying to swallow. "I . . ." but she couldn't go on.

"We can take it back, Livvy." Grandpa grinned. "Get you a different color if you want."

Then she was laughing and crying all at once, shaking her head. She put her hands over her face for a minute and then sniffled back the tears. "This . . ." she choked, "this has been the nicest day of my whole life," and then the tears came pouring down. She lifted her arms for John-Boy and he felt his own throat clogging as he crossed to give her a kiss.

XIII

It was a week John-Boy would never forget. There was still the name *Jenny* in his notebook, and several pages later the sad words he had written when she lay numbed and silent in the bed next to his desk. In the following weeks John-Boy wrote a great deal about the Baldwin sisters and Cousin Homer, and about the night Mama got the washing machine. But it was a long time before he wrote anything more about Jenny. The ending was too abrupt. And too difficult and painful to put into words.

It had come exactly a week after the party at the Baldwin sisters' house. Eula Pendleton had recovered rapidly, and looking back on it, and the fact that Jenny didn't enroll in school the next week, John-Boy guessed he should have known other plans were being made for her. But Jenny had said nothing until that Friday night when she asked him to meet her up on the mountain the next day. John-Boy had laughed at the request. Why should he *meet* her there? If Jenny wanted to go up to the mountain, they could go up together. But

Jenny had insisted—another clue that should have warned him.

The next day, as soon as John-Boy saw her waiting for him he knew it was all over. She was sitting on the hearth of the old fireplace, and her sad smile made words unnecessary. When he sat next to her she handed him a polished dulcimer she was holding tightly in her lap.

"It's for you, John-Boy."

He recognized the instrument immediately: it was the best one Mr. Dawson had ever made. "It's Mr. Dawson's," he said quietly.

"Now it's yours."

John-Boy didn't want to hear the words he knew were coming. But there was no way to avoid it. After a long silence he said, "What made you go and do a thing like that?"

"I wanted to. Because it's ... it's a going-away present."

"I'm not goen anywhere."

It was a beautiful day. A dozen mountain ridges could be seen far to the north, and standing almost stationary above them were huge mounds of billowy white clouds. Fifty years ago John-Boy guessed his great-grandfather must have sat on that same mountaintop admiring the same view. But John-Boy's thoughts were going back only as far as the first night he saw Jenny, that day in church, and those glorious days they had spent discovering the mountain and each other.

"We're leaving today, John-Boy. This afternoon."

John-Boy nodded. "You must have known for days now, Jenny."

There were tears in her eyes. She took his hand, then flung her arms around him. "Oh, John-Boy, I didn't want to ruin it. I wanted us to be happy right up to the end."

"I can't let you go, Jenny. I can't." He kissed her forehead, her eyes and cheeks, and held her tightly.

But they both knew it was impossible. Jenny had to go. And to talk about anything else would only make it more painful. For a long time they held each other in silence.

Jenny finally drew herself away. She looked off at the horizon and then rose and strode to the center of the crumbled room. When she turned around she was smiling, her eyes bright.

"Rome Walton," she said sternly, "now, don't you bring any other old pioneer ladies up here while I'm away!"

John-Boy stared at her for a minute. Then he smiled and came to his feet. "Becky-Lee, you're the only old pioneer lady I ever want."

"I'll expect you to come here and think of me once in a while, Rome Walton." The stern look suddenly softened. "Will you?"

John-Boy took her in his arms again. "You will be in my heart and mind for all enduren time."

"It's breaking my heart to leave you, Rome Walton."

"And mine to see you go, Becky-Lee." John-Boy kissed her again. "I'll come with you, Jenny," he murmured.

"No," she said and then smiled. "Good-bye, old pioneer man."

She turned quickly and moved to the opening where the door had been. There she smiled again, bravely, looking back at him for an instant, and then headed down the mountain.

"Good-bye, Becky-Lee," John-Boy said softly.

ABOUT THE AUTHOR

ROBERT WEVERKA was born in Los Angeles and educated at the University of Southern California, where he majored in economics. His other novels include: *Griff, Search, The Sting, Moonrock, The Widowed Master, One Minute to Eternity* and *I Love My Wife*. He and his family presently live in Idylwild, California.